THE UGLY DUCKLING TURNS

While growing up, Miss Charlotte Forester had repeatedly been informed by her mother that no man would ever want a female as unattractive as she.

But now Charlotte had come of age and into her own. And suddenly every man she met seemed to want her very badly indeed.

Unfortunately one of them was a man who could only be inspired by greed. Another was a rake who seemed to lust rather than love. And the third easily might be a scoundrel whose tender words were as false as the name he gave.

Charlotte was unprepared for so many men wanting her. And still worse, she knew even less about choosing the one she should want. . . .

ABOUT THE AUTHOR

Vanessa Gray grew up in Oak Park, Illinois, and graduated from the University of Chicago. She currently lives in the farm country of northeastern Indiana, where she pursues her interest in the history of Georgian England and the Middle Ages.

Dear Reader:

As you know, Signet is proud to keep bringing you the best in romance and now we're happy to announce that we are now presenting you with even more of what you love!

The Regency has long been one of the most popular settings for romances and it's easy to see why. It was an age of elegance and opulence, of wickedness and wit. It was also a time of tumultuous change, the beginning of the modern age and the end of illusion, when money began to mean as much as birth, but still an age when manners often meant more than morality.

Now Signet has commissioned some of its finest authors to write some bigger romances—longer, lusher, more exquisitely sensuous than ever before—wonderful love stories that encompass even more of the flavor of this glittering and flamboyant age. We are calling them "Super Regencies" because they have been liberated from category conventions and have the room to take the Regency novel even further—to the limits of the Regency itself.

Because we want to bring you only the very best, we are publishing these books only on an occasional basis, only when we feel that we can bring you something special. The first of the Super Regencies, *Love in Disguise* by Edith Layton, was published in August to rave reviews and has won two awards. It was followed by two other outstanding titles, *The Guarded Heart* by Barbara Hazard, published in October and *Indigo Moon* by Patricia Rice, published in February. Watch for future Signet Super Regencies in upcoming months in your favorite bookstore.

Sincerely,

Hilary Ross
Associate Executive Editor

A Lady of Property

Vanessa Gray

A SIGNET BOOK

NEW AMERICAN LIBRARY

SIGNET TRADEMARK U.S. REG. PAT. OFF. AND FOREIGN COUNTRIES
REGISTERED TRADEMARK—MARCA REGISTRADA
HECHO EN CHICAGO, U.S.A.

SIGNET, SIGNET CLASSIC, MENTOR, ONYX, PLUME,
MERIDIAN and NAL BOOKS are published by
NAL PENGUIN INC., 1633 Broadway,
New York, New York 10019

First Printing, April 1988

1 2 3 4 5 6 7 8 9

PRINTED IN THE UNITED STATES OF AMERICA

1

THE DRAWING room at Pentstable seemed, at least to Charlotte Forester, to have shrunk in the last half-hour. Certainly the voices—and Lottie disliked loud voices in the extreme—had swelled in volume and stridency until the walls, covered by fashionable French wallpaper in a misty Egyptian design, seemed to shimmer with the vibrations bombarding them. Even the improbably gray pyramids looked in danger of collapsing onto the tawny sands below.

Lottie's mother, the widowed Lady Forester, had been explaining to her daughters her position on a proposed removal to London. For the last half-hour, Caroline, next eldest to Lottie, had sat uncomfortably straight in her chair, giving a perfect imitation of a faultless daughter, one who, besides being well-behaved, was also possessed of a significant beauty, which would in the near future bring credit to her family.

Lottie, her eyes fixed on a spot in the carpet a few inches from her slippered toes, as usual let her mother's words sweep over her, as the incoming tide washes over a rock. She did not see the sly look cast her way by her sister Caroline, nor the more sympathetic glance from her youngest sister, Amanda.

All she could hear—and even now the sound began to merge into the distance—was her mother's voice.

"It's no use giving you a Season," Lidia Forester said, not for the first time, "for such a plain girl as you

5

has only disappointment to look forward to. The only virtue you possess is your fortune, and why your grandmother left her property to you is more than I can say."

Lottie, moved to defend herself, said mildly, "I was the only grandchild she had then."

"That woman never changed her will, even when Carrie and Amanda came along! No, she favored you, and that's the truth. I suppose if I'd had a son—to be sure, that was not my fault, although your father carried on as though I had produced a daughter on purpose. And how that could have been laid at my door," she continued cryptically, "when he never had a son by that—" She stopped short, contenting herself with merely glowering darkly at the memory of her husband's vulgar inamorata.

She had bred a household of females, and how she would get them all married off creditably, not even to consider *brilliantly*, was more than she could envision.

And adding the last insult to all the other the dowager Lady Forester had heaped upon the head of Lottie's mother, here was Lottie, the most unprepossessing girl she had ever seen, the heiress to that fine estate in the north of England, while her other two daughters had only their faces and a moderate dowry to count on.

Lady Forester at last fell silent. Lottie ventured to abandon the spot on the carpet which had engaged her attention for some time, and met her mother's eyes. She knew only that her mother, as usual, was highly displeased with her. She could not know that every time Lady Forester looked at Lottie, she saw her mother-in-law, and without any effort Lottie's mother felt again the wounding stings of the cutting words, the harmful bruises to her self-esteem that the dowager had dealt her.

Lady Forester had spent a good many wretched years in near proximity to her husband's mother, and she could not but remember them when she looked at

Lottie. To be sure, she tried very hard to be fair. It was not Lottie's fault that her eyes were the exact duplicate of the old lady's, thought Lady Forester not for the first time—very fine greenish eyes, with a deep fringe of lashes, eyes so clear sometimes they appeared transparent. Lady Forester tightened her thin lips until her mouth was a mere slash across her face. The girl was slender, with no figure at all, more like a boy than a young marriageable lady. For the rest, Lady Forester could find nothing to approve. The girl had a great mass of heavy hair, either auburn or brown, depending on how the light caught it. That ugly white streak that lifted like a wing from her left temple—souvenir of a childish attack by a furious Caroline—and that mouth! Far too wide to be attractive in this year of the ladylike rosebud. Fortunately, Lottie did not smile often.

Lottie had long since given up looking in the mirror. She had once shyly traced her resemblance to her formidable grandmother, her features in unaccustomed repose as seen in an oil painting in the large entry hall—promptly banished from the drawing room as soon as the old lady was no more—but she had learned to keep her thoughts to herself.

"Mama," she said now, "truly I shall not mind if Caroline goes into society this year. Pray do not give me any thought. Now, if you will excuse me, I think I feel the headache coming."

Lottie stood up. Her immediate need was a haven where there was no voice pointing out her many faults, where the walls stood more or less still, and where she could indulge in the hearty bout of tears that she felt gathering behind her eyelids.

It was not the first time that Lottie had sought refuge, like a storm-weary sailor, in the spacious bedroom that belonged to her as the eldest daughter. She knew full well that her next sister, Caroline, was waiting, full of hope, until Lottie left home, so that she could claim the bedroom as her own. But if she believed their mother, and there was no reason not to, such an event would be long, long in coming.

Lottie knew, because old Nanny Deming had told her once, when her bout of tears threatened to turn into hysterics, that Lottie was too much like her grandmother for Lady Forester to accept her with any degree of tolerance. And indeed, Lottie thought that might well be the case.

She remembered her paternal grandmother with a good deal of affection. The dowager petted her, took her side of things, and believed her tales implicitly. Lottie was too young, and Nanny not wise enough, to know that the dowager had hated Lottie's mother from the first day her son announced that he wanted to marry her. No lady would have been fit to touch even the tail of her son's Weston-tailored coat, at least in her eyes, and she blamed her son's untimely death not on the horse that threw him over a hedge into a ditch, but in some intangible way on his widow. And the present Lady Forester remembered all too well a series of harrowing scenes, interspersed with innumerable small but hurtful pricks, ending only with the dowager's death ten years before.

Lottie's mother was really fond of her eldest daughter, but she could not see any need of expressing her affection, even if she could have found words. Every time she was aware of a rush of emotion toward her daughter, she saw the straight eyebrows, the deep-set green eyes, the slender unfeminine body—and there was the spiteful dowager facing her again.

Now, upstairs in her bedroom, Lottie closed the door firmly behind her and leaned back against it. In truth, she could not see clearly across the room, for her eyes were full of unshed tears. She knew she was not pretty—only her grandmother had ever approved of her looks, and then in such terms as to make the compliment excessively dubious.

"You're not in the fashion, Lottie. Not your namby-pamby washed-out, die-away blonds, that is certain. Nor enough curves in the right places. In fact," the dowager finished with glee, "you're so much like me that you'll have to count on your character to make your way. Character's the thing, child. It lasts forever, while looks change with years, and with fashion if you please. Character brings you everything you need."

Lottie remembered that conversation very well, though she had been only eight years old. Her grandmother had looked about her with enormous satisfaction, at the very comfortable bedroom, where she was assiduously waited upon by her dear Montgomery. Then, turning back to her favorite grandchild, she added, "You'll do fine, Lottie. I saw to that years ago, when you were in your cradle. You'll have Pomfret."

The old lady had given her sharp crow of laughter, and Lottie, even at her young age, had detected a kind of triumph in it. "You've nothing of your mother in you. You're another Adelia Granville, and don't forget it!"

At this moment, to be an Adelia Granville was not an enviable goal. Unless, of course, one wished to be free of all the world's cares, as Grandmother was. But surely there was another way!

Sometime later, Lottie's eyes had cleared. Tears were never the answer, and she did not cry often. Now it was time to consider what might lie ahead of her. If a London Season and an accompanying offer of advantageous marriage were out of the question, then what alternative was available?

Governess? Companion to a crotchety old lady? A disrespectful thought touched her. She was already in that position! Go to London and become a clerk in a shop?

Go to Pomfret?

It was suddenly as though she heard her grand-mother's voice in her ear. "You'll do fine, Lottie—I've seen to that!"

She would go to Pomfret!

Pomfret now belonged to Lottie. It had been her grandmother's home when she was young Adelia Gran-ville, before she married Grandfather. Lottie had never seen her inheritance, but she knew approximately where it lay, north and perhaps a little west. Someone had said once it was not far off the Great North Road, and as a child Lottie had fixed it on the globe as lying somewhere near the Orkney Islands, beyond the boundary of the civilized world. Later, she learned it was only in the north of England and, while remote, was perfectly accessible.

But Lottie held fast to the estate, and still allowed an elderly Granville cousin with little means to live in the Priory, along with a suitable staff of servants. Although she thought of it—at least to this point—only four times a year when the quarterly remittance arrived, she realized that she was thinking more and more about the property as providing a welcome bolt hole.

She knew that if she removed to the Priory, she would be confessing that there was no chance for a life in society, or even a life of normal social exchanges. She knew, vaguely, that the Priory was far from any civilized town, and she would grow old and queer in solitary eremitic life . . .

Besides, she thought practically, owning no carriage of her own, how could she get there?

A quick rap on the door came, followed immediately by the entrance of her mother. "Lottie? I had not finished what I had planned to say."

"No need to finish," said Lottie, her voice sounding oddly muffled to her.

"I think it is time," said Lady Forester, paying no heed to her daughter's response, "that we consider Caroline's future. As I told you, I shall wish to hire a house in town in the fall—the Little Season, you know. Pray do not give in to a fit of the sulks, for I shall need you to help me with all the arrangements. There will be such a to-do—so much to do, I declare it will quite drive me mad! I recall my own first Season—gowns, and gloves, and flowers, and feathers, and hairdressers—"

"Never having been in London, I should not in the least know how to go on," said Lottie in a flat, unaccented voice. "I shall be of no use at all."

"But you will learn, my dear. I have a few friends left in town, and I am sure they will inform us as to the latest fashions and the persons who are quite *au fait*, and proper to invite to Carrie's first ball." Lady Forester crossed to take the chair opposite Lottie. "I have come to the most exciting decision!"

Lottie turned her clear green gaze on her mother. Lady Forester did not quite like the speculative quality in that level look, reminding her forcefully again of Waldo's mother.

"Truly I have," Lady Forester resumed, not quite so optimistically as before. "With a Season's experience, you will be able to move in society with assurance, and I see you—in my mind's eye, of course—as a lady of quality in great demand. For showing young ladies and their mamas just how to go on, don't you know. And you could name your own price, of course—you have no idea just how some of these country people long for someone to show them what to do, and of course with the cits coming into society from time to time . . ."

Her voice died away. She saw no spark of response on her daughter's features. Her great idea was being spurned without so much as a word being said.

She stood up, shaking herself like a ruffled peahen. "I should have thought you would be grateful for the idea, Lottie. I vow I do not know quite what to do with you!"

Compunction touched Lottie. She rose too, and kissed her mother lightly on the cheek. "Pray do not worry, Mama. We must get Carrie married off, and then Amanda. And then we will see what to do about me."

In a quick and unaccustomed glimpse of the truth, Lady Forester said, "I doubt not that I shall be glad of your company, at the end."

She left, and Lottie sank back into her low thoughts. At the end! Glad of her company at the end? It was clear that Lottie's company would be welcomed for her function, not for herself, before that grim time. At the end. The phrase, with an apocalyptic overtone, echoed in her thoughts for the rest of the day.

At the same time that day, a gentleman of whose existence Lottie was as yet unaware sat in his rooms in Duke Street and considered in which of the directions available to him lay the most promising path to his future.

Marcus North considered himself staid and prosy. Well-educated according to the current standards of a cultivated man, he had attended Oxford along with his cousin Geoffrey Lassiter, had donned the stuff gown of the ordinary undergraduate, choosing not to wear the gold-tasseled cap and silk gown of the gentleman commoner. He might have claimed that privilege, for he was well-connected, but he was modest to a fault.

He knew well that his appearance was not that of an Adonis, as he stood barely above middle height. His shoulders, however, were broad and his torso powerful, as many a young gentleman attending Jackson's Gym could attest.

Being an only child of parents long deceased, he had little practice in dealing with ladies of quality. In truth, his ambitions lay rather along the lines of the leisurely life of a country gentleman of more than adequate fortune, which he was—but also that of domesticity, with sons and daughters rising up around him to banish the loneliness of his life as an orphan. This latter felicity had not so far come his way. Hence, his present prolonged visit to London.

At this moment, Geoffrey Lassiter was ringing a peal over him. "Good God, Marcus, I thought you came to London to find a wife! You've had six months to survey the field. Don't you see anything you fancy?"

Geoffrey held a small position in an obscure government office at which he worked spasmodically, but sufficiently to justify his continued residence in London. Now he sat in Marcus' sitting room opposite his cousin and regarded him with affectionate exasperation.

"Not to say fancy, Geoff," said Marcus slowly. "I daresay one or two might do, but do you know, I can't quite see any of these eligible ladies at Gresham Manor. They are so at home here in these great mob scenes that pass for parties! I can't bring myself to offer for a female who abhors even touching her dainty foot to the green earth, to say nothing of enjoying it!"

"You surely don't expect Annabella, for instance—that female I've seen you with—to roam your lanes with a pair of spaniels at her heels, when there is all London to amuse her?"

Marcus reddened. "But that is what I do want, Geoff. But how to broach the subject? I confess that is quite beyond me!"

Geoff gave a short bark of laughter. "You mean you don't want to be turned down. Well, I can't blame you for that. I'll tell you, Marcus, I wish I had been turned down at least once more than I was."

The tone in his voice startled Marcus and he looked sharply at his cousin. Besides being related, each was probably the best friend the other had. Growing up together, going to Oxford, even separated for some months at a time, yet each was sustained by the thought that somewhere was a friend he could count on to the death.

Marcus dared not speak. If Geoff wished to confide in him, he would. After a long moment, Geoff continued. "I think you're right, Marcus. You always had more sense than I did. Don't go for surface prettiness. Don't listen to all the good things her friends tell you about her. Any girl's mama will praise her to the skies, but only along the lines you want to hear. You'll never be told the girl hasn't enough brains to find her way out of a drawing room. Or that she will reveal—after you are married, of course—an active dislike of dogs, especially your favorite spaniels, and scream the house down if one so much as touches her hand with his nose. Nor will you know that she is determined to cultivate the most scandalous gossip of the year, even if she manages not to be the subject of it, and that she will run up bills all over town sufficient to finance the war with Napoleon. And yet I think we might rub along well enough were it not for her mama. Lady Monteagle *cannot* refrain from interfering in everything that catches her eye! I wish she could find someone else to harry!"

Geoff's unexpected tirade ended. A pulsating silence fell between the two men. Geoff, as though wound so tightly he must explode in physical action, rose and strode restlessly to the window, turning his back on the room. Marcus was embarrassed, not at the unexpected confidence, but at the realization that he could not help.

"Never mind, Marcus," said Geoff, forcing a smile, "nothing you can do. And at the time I did think I had found my ideal woman. No one could have changed my mind then. Not even you."

"I'm sorry."

"I started out, you know, to tell you whom to marry. Annabella, perhaps, if you're taken with her. At least three ladies would, I know, be willing to accept your offer. At least my wife tells me so, and I must admit she is likely right."

"Three? I should not have thought even one."

"I withdraw all my advice, Marcus. Surely you can do far better on your own than to take any suggestions of mine. But you know it is time to marry."

"Well, of course. After all, that's why I'm in London."

Marcus was reluctant to admit that London and its society were a great disappointment to him. By all accounts, if one could not find a bride in London, then one could not find a bride at all. Stunned, however, by the glimpse he had just been given of Geoff's unhappy match, he wondered whether marriage was required of him after all.

Geoff, turning from the window where he had been looking down at the slow traffic in Duke Street, said on a whimsical note, "Don't let me put you off marriage. Not all matches, I believe, are unhappy. But . . . can you accept one word of advice?"

"Absolutely. Even two," said Marcus, trying to match his cousin's mood.

"Marry for property. Then at least you'll have the land, if nothing else."

After Geoff left, Marcus turned over in his mind his dilemma. If his future had not been uncertain before Geoff's confidences, it certainly was now. Three ladies ready to marry him? Unbelievable! They were after his property—they must be. A substantial fortune lay in his hands, and indeed at Gresham Manor his income could be considered munificent, even though in London it would not go so far.

He had been hoping, he now realized, for a tender and sweet meeting in London. Where had that romantic streak of his come from? Never had he considered himself anything but conventional to a fault, unimaginative, dismissing passion as an illusion. But now that he allowed his thoughts to run as they would, he was conscious of acute disappointment that Geoff's marriage—which he had in a way envied—was a failure.

If Geoff had not been able to find happiness with his lady, one of the most gorgeously provocative blonds Marcus had ever seen, then what chance had he?

The depressing thought kept him company all through that day and into the next. While he was mildly curious as to the identity of the three ladies—three!—he preferred, he thought, not to know.

2

SOME FEW days after his unsettling conversation with his cousin, Marcus North found himself at Devonshire House, where the duchess was having a small entertainment, only a couple of hundred persons, barely enough to keep the enormous house from seeming empty.

Marcus had been given much to think about. If Geoffrey found his mother-in-law too interfering, remedies were at hand. Of course, one could hardly forbid the lady the house, or exile her to the country, especially since Lady Monteagle, the dowager in question, was possessed of a good deal of wealth at her own disposal, in addition to the estate entailed on some second cousin.

Geoffrey might well, supposing he were not entangled with a government office, retire to his country home, where there was room to escape daily into the affairs of the farms.

Marcus' second thought was more personal. Suppose he offered for Annabella? She would have a substantial dowry, she had an appealing childlike pout when she was disappointed, and she clearly had a *tendre* for Marcus.

But . . . there was her mother.

And, quite frankly, Annabella was not worth the trouble of dealing with her mother. Even though Marcus was not even close to offering for Annabella, Geoffrey had given him much to think about.

He had come alone to Devonshire House. Perhaps he would see Annabella there. But he was suddenly acutely aware that he had escorted her in public much too often recently, and it should have been no surprise that the *ton* were convinced he would soon offer.

And perhaps, in the long run, he might. But not tonight.

He entered the great doors of the house on Portugal Street, held open by liveried footmen, and found his way to the great public rooms upstairs. He greeted friends, spoke in friendly but noncommittal fashion to Annabella, who chided him for not calling on her, and greeted her mother politely but briefly.

Some time passed before he arrived at the far end of the salon. A gambling game was being played in one of the smaller rooms, and ordinarily he might risk a few sovereigns, but tonight he was too restless to take an interest. He was not a gambler at heart, and it appalled him to think of risking thousands of pounds on the throw of a pair of dice.

He turned back at the door to the small room, and his gaze fell on the last person he wanted to see. An urge to flee came over him, but flight was impossible. Geoffrey's mother-in-law had fixed her sharp gaze on him and he was trapped as thoroughly as a butterfly on a pin.

"There you are," announced Lady Monteagle, with an eye to the obvious. "I haven't seen you this dog's age. Come and sit down by me."

He obliged her and said a few courteous words.

"But that's not what I want to hear," she told him in her raspy voice.

Lady Monteagle was aptly named. Bent with age, she sat with shoulders hunched, staring out from her bold-featured face on a world she did not much admire. Her fierce unblinking eyes darted from one to another of those around her, much like a bird of prey scanning the ground beneath him for rodents.

She was not an amiable old lady. Only those who had known her for a long time were aware of the great kindness that lurked beneath the formidable exterior—and even those, like Geoffrey, tended to forget that fact, hidden as it was under layers of apparent and usually vocal contempt.

But one always listened to the old lady, because there was meat in her comments. So it was now, Marcus realized with a start.

"Now, then, young Marcus, what is this I hear about your going to offer for that blond chit?"

"I don't know what you mean." Even to Marcus, his words limped sadly.

"I mean that Annabella Fitzhugh. And don't try to bam me. You know what I mean."

Marcus had not made up his mind yet about Annabella. But his decision ought to be his own, and not Lady Monteagle's. He said, "She is a beauty, is she not? And I understand a good bit of fortune comes with her." Marcus grinned to himself and added, "For the fortunate bridegroom."

As he expected, his companion snorted explosively. "Fortune! What do you need of fortune? Especially when a total nincompoop comes with it! You think she'd be happy at Gresham Manor? Where gossip often comes six months late, and the latest fashions even later?"

"A country life is a good one," said Marcus calmly. "I suspect she will take to it easily." He glanced sideways at the old lady.

But she was not amused. "I think you are attempting to fun me, young Marcus. Don't forget I dandled you on my knee before you were out of leading strings!"

That was indeed true, but there had been long years

after his parents died during which he had seen nothing of their old friends. Not until Geoffrey had married Maria had Lady Monteagle come into his ken again.

"I tell you," the old lady was going on, "she'll lead you a pretty chase! Not a thought in that fluffy head! No, Marcus, it will not do. Besides, just imagine that vixen settling in at Gresham! No, no, I cannot believe you would be happy."

"Vixen?" echoed Marcus faintly. Annabella was many things, but vixen he would not accept.

"Lady Fitzhugh, of course," said his companion impatiently. "She knows a good thing when she sees it!"

"Why do I feel," suggested Marcus wryly, "like a prize bullock on the sale block?"

"Because," said Lady Monteagle smartly, "that's what you are. Did you think only young ladies paraded around London on display to make good marriages? Don't think their mamas are sitting idly by, not a bit of it!"

Startled, Marcus exclaimed, "Do you mean I have been sized up by all those ladies out there?" He gestured vaguely. "Suppose I have been found wanting?"

She gave the short bark that passed for laughter with her. "The mamas are looking at security for their daughters. The man himself is hardly noticed until after the vows."

"But suppose the bridegroom is a monster?"

"Then the young lady produces a son, which is her duty, and she may then lead a life of her own."

He was silent for a few moments, thinking dark thoughts. He had truly been aware of the crass materialism which ruled the marriage arrangements of the upper classes. And, for all he knew, of the lower classes as well. But trust Lady Monteagle to put it harshly and unequivocally.

His idealism struggled to the surface. "Surely there

must be a lady who reads books? Who likes the country? With an amiable disposition?''

"Of course," said Lady Monteagle. "I myself was such a one."

"Well, at least Annabella is a biddable young lady," said Marcus, wondering how he had allowed himself to fall into such a very strange conversation.

Lady Monteagle had entered into this *tête-à-tête* with firm purpose. She had no intention of allowing Lady Fitzhugh to establish any rights over Gresham Manor. It was a pretty country seat, and the Norths, being beforehand with the world and thus able to afford comfort, had always maintained a high standard of household service. She herself had visited there in the past couple of years with Geoffrey and her daughter, and enjoyed herself thoroughly. And since she loathed Annabella's mother, she was determined to put a spoke in the wheel of that lady's plans.

Marcus, acutely conscious of Geoffrey's complaints about his mother-in-law, could see even more clearly than Lady Monteagle herself the perils that lay in wait for the husband of Annabella Fitzhugh.

"Well, then, Lady Monteagle," said Marcus, attempting to bring this uncomfortable meeting to a close with commendable raillery, "perhaps you have such a lady in mind for me? One who perhaps has not yet burst on the London market—I mean, *scene*?"

Lady Monteagle stunned him. "Yes, as a matter of fact I have. At least, I think so."

He stared at her, unbelieving. "You have?"

"Long ago," said Lady Monteagle, "when we were both girls, my good friend Lidia Worley married a baronet, Sir Waldo Forester. His mother was a witch, Lidia always said, and made her life unpleasant in the extreme. But she's a widow now, and has daughters—no sons. I think the eldest one—"

"I don't think so." Marcus suddenly found the whole

subject distasteful. "I had best do my own searching."

"Don't be an idiot. How do you think marriages are arranged? Let me at least write and see whether there's a chance that the eldest girl will be in London soon. *Then* you can do your own choosing."

Marcus needed some convincing. His companion, nothing loath, set herself to bring all her armament to bear. "Perhaps you remember the girl? She's old Adelia Granville's granddaughter. Aha, I see that caught your interest. Yes, indeed. Lidia told me once that the girl inherited Pomfret. Is that not near Gresham?"

"We share a boundary line. But I don't remember any granddaughters. In truth, I hardly remember Lady Forester—the dowager, I mean."

"No, of course you wouldn't. When she married Forester, she moved down to his place. After he died, she stayed on in the house, making life miserable for Lidia. But she's dead now, as is her son. Let me write—"

Marcus protested earnestly. "No, no. If by chance the young lady comes to London, then we'll see. Lady Monteagle, do not write on my behalf. Whatever you say, I shall deny it!"

After another few moments of conversation, Marcus left the lady, feeling assured that he had dissuaded her from her purpose. However, he did not read correctly the spark in the old lady's eyes—the unmistakable sign of a born matchmaker. Geoffrey would have recognized that glint, but he would have translated it as "her confounded propensity for meddling."

Marcus certainly did not want anyone to choose a wife for him. Not that he had his mind made up, and if there were indeed a young lady of intelligence and education, and he might meet her in the ordinary way, he might well accept what the fates brought him.

Of course, since Marcus was no different from many another English gentleman, he spared a few moments to consider the advantage of adding Pomfret Priory, supposing it to be the unknown lady's dowry, to his own lands.

Lady Monteagle, ignoring Marcus' urgent pleas for her to forget her suggestion, sat at her desk late that night. She had not seen Lidia Forester for some time, but they had maintained a desultory correspondence over the years that the latter had been immured in the country. There was no need for Lady Monteagle to mend epistolary fences, but it would do no harm to choose her words carefully.

"About time for you to bring your eldest daughter to London . . . I am sure you recognize . . ." No, that wasn't quite right. She tried again. "I quite long to see your eldest daughter. She must have grown into a charming young lady. . . . By the oddest chance I am well-acquainted with my son-in-law's cousin, Marcus North. His country home is Gresham Manor. Is that not quite near the dowager's childhood home? He is in London and cuts quite a swath among the young belles. I should so like to tell him about your Charlotte . . ."

There was, of course, much more in the newsy letter, but Lady Monteagle had no doubt that Lady Forester could winkle out the pertinent paragraph. To a knowledgeable woman—and she knew Lidia Forester to be so —the words between the lines were as clear as those written, and far more legible, since Lady Monteagle wrote in a fashionably crabbed hand.

Lady Forester was up to the mark. Her friend's letter cast all her plans for Carrie into chaos.

"Do you know," she said to Lottie, unfortunately in Carrie's hearing, "I believe you ought to have your Season. Who knows but what you might catch the fancy of a suitor after all?"

Lottie stared at her suspiciously. "What is in that letter, Mama?"

Carrie roared in outrage. "What's the use of a Season for Lottie? You said she'd never take! Do I have to wait around a *whole year* for Lottie to—"

"To what?" demanded Lottie, turning on her sister. "Get out of your way?"

"Now, Lottie . . . Carrie. It is just that—"

Lady Forester realized she had already lost this battle. Carrie was counting on her Season, and she had every right to, since Lady Forester herself had decreed it. But she was determined not to lose the war.

"Lady Monteagle has written to say that Lottie must come to London—"

"For a Season?" Lottie was aghast. "She has not set eyes on me for years. I faintly recall her visiting, but why does she take an interest in me now?" She added silently: Now that I have grown up so plain?

Lady Forester found no easy way to mention Marcus North, but at last Lady Monteagle's message was out.

"You have already made arrangements for me to . . . to captivate some man I have never seen? Really, Mama—"

"But what about me?" wailed Carrie. "My gowns are being made, and . . . and *it is my Season*!"

Lottie ignored her sister. "So it will be like this—I have a Season after all? I will be put through my paces like a pony at the Horse Fair, and if I pass inspection, then the great Mr. Whatever will deign to consider me? What if he finds me unsound of wind and limb? Will he send me back? No, Mama, I do not think I shall go to London."

This was a side of Lottie that her mother had never suspected, and now that it had risen to the surface, it both surprised and dismayed Lady Forester. She could not see that Lottie's hidden fears of being rejected, fostered by the long years when her mother had done just that, even though unwittingly, had burst into the open.

Later that morning, when Carrie's tears and Lottie's anger had spent themselves, Lady Forester considered her conscience. Lottie, in her opinion, was truly so plain as to be unmarriageable, and that assessment was unchanged. Further, she dared not take a chance on Lottie's bolting, like the pony she had mentioned. And of course, suppose Mr. North did not like what he saw? The whole Season, if Lottie's, would be wasted, Lottie would be disappointed, and they would all have suffered a year of Carrie's sulks. Lady Forester shuddered at the thought.

But if Lottie went to London, in Carrie's train as it were, then perhaps Mr. North could be persuaded to call. The dreadful thought came to her: perhaps he would prefer Carrie, and the fat would be in the fire for certain. No, Lottie must come out into society alone. But how to arrange it all?

Lady Forester had no doubt of her ability to persuade Lottie to come around in the end. She sat down to respond to her friend's letter: "My dear Lottie has generously decided to forgo her own Season for the moment to give her sister Caroline the opportunity . . . plans too far forward to change . . . but Lottie will be in London and will be at home to Mr. North." Then, as a kind of insurance against anyone's disappointment, she added, "Lottie looks much like her Grandmother Forester."

Lady Monteagle had no trouble in translating Lidia's letter. The second daughter ruled the roost at Pentstable. But she wonderd whether Lottie might be an antidote. Not, she decided, if she looks like old Lady Forester, Adelia Granville in her youth—Lady Monteagle well remembered *that* legend.

Well, if Lidia did not wish to marry her eldest daughter to a man of some wealth, it was not Lady

Monteagle's chore to do it for her. But then, a day after she received the letter, she caught another glimpse of Annabella Fitzhugh and her ubiquitous mother. Visualizing them at Gresham Manor, Lady Monteagle mentally girded up her loins to do battle, not necessarily on behalf of Lottie, but primarily to do Lady Fitzhugh a mischief.

Further correspondence, in the next fortnight, flew between London and Pentstable. Lady Forester now moved cautiously. She had not Lottie's acquiescence, but expected to prevail. Lady Monteagle not only read into Lidia's letters more than was there but also herself was in no way averse to embroidering fancifully on the truth.

Marcus was appalled to learn that Lady Monteagle had embarked on the correspondence that he had negated at the start. The more she elaborated on the charms of the young lady, however, the more he began to weaken. He was disenchanted with the ladies he knew in London. Perhaps an unknown—someone of intelligence and amiable disposition, as Lady Monteagle had described her—might be interesting.

He was wary of falling into Lady Monteagle's trap. However, matrimony would be the end of it, whether the trap were baited with the blond Annabella or the mysterious Miss Forester. He must marry, being a man who saw his duty clearly, and the sooner all was settled, the sooner he could go home to Gresham.

Lady Monteagle had told him, untruthfully, that Miss Forester was anxious to receive him in London. But still, intrigued but cautious, he did not wish to follow along the lines Geoffrey's mother-in-law had laid down.

He found a royal solution to his dilemma. Wasn't it the eighth Henry who had leapt astride his steed and traveled to Dover to get a preview of one of his brides? Perhaps it was Charles the Second, but no matter. If it worked for a king, then it would do the same for a mere gentleman.

Summoning his groom, Irving, he gave instructions. In due course, he set out in his curricle, Irving beside him, driving his chestnuts on the road to the north. His destination was Pentstable. He had no doubt of his welcome, for had not Lady Monteagle prepared the way for him? He would meet the young lady and make his decision then. If he found her an antidote, he could easily refrain from calling on her in London.

He set out in the briskness of a bright morning, his confidence high, and his spirits, raised by recognition of his own acumen in planning this preliminary and non-committal meeting, remarkably cheerful.

3

THE PENTSTABLE household was humming along, busy as only a household can be when preparing for a purposeful descent on London.

Miss Doughty, the seamstress from the village, and Nancy, her assistant, had taken up temporary residence in the house—under the roof on the third floor, to be sure, among the servants, but at least the women were spared the long daily drive to their cottage in the village. Bolts of muslin, satin, and linen in the most romantic rainbow colors spilled over the table in the sewing room, and wispy lengths of gauze spangled with gold and silver shimmered on the shelves.

Carrie gave herself airs far beyond her station, as her younger sister, Amanda, pointed out more frequently than was strictly necessary. At length even Lady Forester was moved to reprimand her favorite daughter.

"I do not wonder that Miss Wythe gave up on you," said Lady Forester at last. "Try as she would, she told me, she could not make a lady out of you."

"Lottie was always her favorite." Carrie pouted. "I could do nothing right for the old dragon."

"But Lottie never abused servants. I cannot believe you speak to Miss Doughty the way you do. I vow, Caroline, unless you settle down and allow Miss Doughty to finish these gowns, you may find yourself in London with naught to wear."

At least I would be in London, thought Carrie. I'd manage somehow.

As though she were privy to her daughter's thoughts, Lady Forester added, "You are not quite the Princess Regent yet, you know. I shall be surprised if the Prince takes any notice of a young and green girl. You will be well-advised to act the demure miss, even if you feel that no young lady ever went to London before. Carrie, I have half a mind not to bring you out in London after all." At the wail that came from her second daughter, she relented. "At least until next year, supposing you have learned a little decorum in the meantime." Then, to emphasize her point, she added deliberately, "I wonder whether Miss Wythe is occupied at the moment. She might be willing to return and teach you how to go on."

Lottie could have informed her mother as to Miss Wythe's whereabouts, for she had kept up a steady correspondence with her former governess. The mention of Miss Wythe struck Lottie as a fortuitous incident. She had been thinking along lines that would have struck her mother as outrageous, and in fact Lottie herself shrank from entertaining prospects of which she could not see the outcome clearly. But Miss Wythe might well be the factor she had been looking for.

While Carrie stormed to her room in a strong fit of pique, Lottie considered Miss Wythe. Her governess, a gentlewoman in reduced circumstances, and Lottie found they had much in common, and Lottie considered her former governess as perhaps her best friend in the world. If, as seemed likely, her own future lay along the lines of a career as lady's companion or governess, she could do no better than to model herself on her dear Miss Wythe.

Her mother's earlier suggestion that both she, Lottie, might set herself up as an adviser to young maidens ready to burst upon society was totally out of the question. Lottie suspected, rightly, that her mother had already dismissed the idea from her mind.

But of course any possibilities lay well in the future. First, she must assist in getting Carrie married, and then, in all likelihood, Amanda as well. The years stretched ahead in somber fashion. Interminable days and weeks on the fringe of London society, watching Carrie pirouette and curtsy, looking coyly from the corners of her eyes—as Lottie had caught the girl in rehearsal before a mirror—listening to tales of a society her mother had told her she was too plain to join: it was not a pretty prospect.

But at the moment, there was Carrie, demanding the full attention of everyone in the house, and Lottie's thoughts were fully occupied.

Lady Forester felt at sea. She had not envisioned Lottie as having a defiant bone in her body. She believed the girl, so much like her grandmother in appearance, to be as biddable as the old lady had not been. The Lottie she looked at now was a stranger. And Lady Forester thought she had made a dangerous mistake in broaching the matter of Mr. North in such an offhand fashion when she received the first letter from Fenella Monteagle. It was too late to amend that, but at least she was still Lottie's mother, and Lottie would do as she said.

With renewed confidence she explained what she knew. "The man is from the north someplace. Odd, with a name like that, isn't it? Although I suppose someone in Scotland might consider him as coming from the south. No matter. The man owns Gresham Manor, a fine property, and likely an income to match. The Norths were always beforehand with the world, and certainly you will want for nothing. I wonder which branch of the family he resembles? The Norths, being next neighbors, were great friends of your grandmother as a girl—"

She stopped short. Her daughter, standing in the doorway, was pale as bleached linen, and that strange streak of white hair rising like a wing from her temple seemed merely an extension of her pallor.

Too late she saw that she had blundered. Lottie was no fool.

"So," breathed Lottie, to her mother's great dismay, "he wants Pomfret to add to his property. He does not even want me as a female. He wants my land. Well, he shall not have it!"

In a flash of gray muslin skirt, she was gone, leaving her mother to contemplate the wrack of breakfast without seeing it, aware only that she had a good deal of persuasive work ahead of her. Much as she was irritated with Carrie and her frivolous airs, just now, compared with Lottie, she considered her second child a paragon among daughters.

Lady Forester's thoughts, having risen to such heights of rejoicing only moments ago, now plunged heavily to the ground.

If only Lottie weren't so plain! That flat figure—so much like a boy's! That odd streak of white hair, like a wing sweeping upward, and adding—so Lady Forester considered—a good ten years to her age!

Well, the girl would simply have to be brought to an acceptance of the duty she owed her family. If there were the slightest chance for a match, Lottie would receive the gentleman sponsored by Lady Monteagle. There was not the slightest doubt of that!

Lottie had more than a slight doubt.

At about the same time that Marcus North set out from London on what might be termed a journey of discovery, Lady Forester believed it appropriate to address herself again to persuading Lottie into a more amiable frame of mind.

Lottie was unyielding. "It's useless to meet anyone. I have decided, Mama, that I shall never marry."

"Not marry?" Lady Forester's voice rose in a manner that in the ordinary way would have sounded the tocsin in her daughter's mind. "I do not like to remind you," she said, ignoring the many times she had already mentioned the topic, "that you are not in the way of receiving very many offers."

Without volition, Lottie heard herself saying, "I might do if I were to go to London, even for the Little Season."

She had never expected to bare her own deepest wish, especially to her mother, who as a fast rule made light of Lottie's hopes. Lady Forester did not recognize the wistful sadness in Lottie's voice.

"But, my dear, you know you would be cast in the shade by Carrie. Her golden curls, her blue eyes—quite in the current mode, you know, and she must take advantage of it before raven tresses and snapping black eyes comes back into fashion." Her tone of voice left no doubt that Lottie's kind of looks were best kept in the shires, and never brought into the bright beam of London society.

"Then, Mama, you agree," said Lottie in a strangled voice, "that the man simply wants to add to Gresham Manor, by marriage? Why else would he want to meet me? I can see you agree. Well, then, I have thought about this, and I pray you will write to Lady Monteagle that I will sell Pomfret Priory to him, but I shall not receive him."

"It can do no harm to meet the man, Lottie. I declare I cannot fathom your objections."

Nor did Lottie herself fully understand her dread of meeting the man. She was aware that Lady Monteagle had all but offered—on Mr. North's behalf, of course—marriage. Lottie could not know that Lady Monteagle had long since lost her grip on facts pertaining to Marcus North. But Lottie entertained a healthy fund of good sense, and she had her doubts about the entire business.

Gently she said, "Mama, let us speak no more of this. It is Carrie's Season, not mine." *Never* mine, she told herself. Lottie's chin quivered. Her mother could not, through the tears suddenly flooding her own eyes, detect her daughter's distress.

Lottie, their roles reversed, put her arm around her mother's shaking shoulders and led her to a chair. Kneeling beside her mother, she set herself to comfort her with soothing sounds, but all the time she knew that nothing but total capitulation to her mother's wishes could bring them again to harmony—if not harmony, Lottie amended, then at least to a truce.

But that capitulation Lottie could not bring herself to make.

In the ensuing days, Lady Forester returned again and again to the attack.

"Lottie, you must realize how advantageous marriage can be."

"But no one has offered marriage."

Ignoring this, Lady Forester continued. "A woman can only gain respect in the world by her marriage."

"But I respect myself, Mama."

A twist of her mother's lips told Lottie how little that argument weighed in the scales. "You will always be the odd one in society. Dinners are planned for couples, you know, and while your friends may invite you to their little gatherings, at least for a while, soon you will find that your name has been crossed off their invitation lists, unless there is such a press that you can be lost in the crowd."

"I cannot think my friends would desert me so."

"Not that we have so many here, after all." Inspiration struck Lady Forester. "You recall your Great-Aunt

Clotilde? Ah, I see you do. Well, my child,'' she added dryly, "there you may see yourself in a dozen years' time.''

Although she did not know it, she had struck the one note that could evoke a response from Lottie. Great-Aunt Clotilde was a crabbed hermit of a woman, eccentric to the point that if she had not had a fortune she might well have found herself in Bedlam. As it was, she was shunned by all who knew her, and left her home only to take the waters at Bath once a year.

And Lottie recognized at last the choice that lay directly ahead of her. She would either go into service as a governess to children not her own, until she withered like unripe fruit on a vine, wrinkled and sour, or become a recluse like Great-Aunt Clotilde.

Lady Forester had at last summoned up a response, even though silent, from Lottie. But the response was not precisely what Lady Forester had had in mind.

"Well?'' she demanded, "I think that now you will see where your duty lies. I knew you would come to your senses sooner or later. But I do promise you this, Lottie. If you find him totally repugnant to you''—and her tone suggested that Lottie, if she knew what was good for her, would find him no such thing—"then I shall not insist that you see him again. But you must receive at least.''

But Lottie, lost in her thoughts that had suddenly begun to move with purpose, scarcely heard her mother's promise.

As the time appointed for their departure for London drew near, Lottie realized that if she accompanied her family she would—willy-nilly—find herself in a drawing room of their hired house, receiving Mr. North.

It was possible that, had the encounter been presented more casually to her, she would have agreed. After all, one meeting was hardly significant. But her self-esteem, never more than minimal, had taken a battering recently, and could now only lash out in protest.

Her only hope, and it was a desperate one, was negative. She would not go to London!

She began to plan. The day before the family was to leave for London, she must be on her own way in the opposite direction. She must take the coach to the market town of Alford, where her dear Miss Wythe, paragon among governesses, lived. She would find shelter there.

Lottie had not thought beyond the haven of Miss Wythe's cottage. It seemed reasonable to expect a mind of hue and cry to be raised by Lady Forester, and she was prepared to weather that storm. But at least she would not be required to meet Mr. North, to see him face-to-face knowing that he measured her not in terms of feminine charm but in acres owned.

If all else failed—and Lottie had a shrewd idea that she would be harried even at Alford until she was forced to meet Lady Monteagle's young protégé—she would go to her own place. Pomfrey Priory was hers, and she would live there, not alone, for the elderly Granville cousin could not be turned out.

No matter how isolated Pomfret might be, no matter how unpleasant the company of her cousin might prove, yet her situation must be better than it was at present.

4

M R. MARCUS North arrived at Pentstable on the third day of his journey. The roads up from London had proved to be in better condition than he had anticipated, the heavy rains of last week having bypassed this corner of Hertfordshire. Later in the summer, the passage of wheels, even of pedestrians' feet, would raise clouds of dust that could be seen across the fields for a mile or more, not only coating the horses and the carriage but also seeping through the leather curtains and coating the passengers with a tawny layer of grit.

Marcus could have made the journey in two days instead of the three and a half he had estimated, had he set the smart pace of which his cattle were capable. He might also have bypassed the village inn, such as it was. He would, no doubt, have been made welcome by Lady Forester, judging from Lady Monteagle's report of her correspondence with her friend.

He drew up to the sweep before the grand entrance to Pentstable. As Marcus stepped to the ground, he was aware of a twitching curtain at a window to the right of the main entrance. Ahead of him in the next few moments, he realized belatedly, was quite the hardest thing he had ever done. If he were to yield to impulse, he would be away down the drive in minutes.

Slowly he mounted the three steps to the entrance and announced himself. Suppose Lady Monteagle had lied? Suppose Miss Forester was a complete antidote? Protruding teeth, or a serious lisp in her speech? A vapid demeanor? Even, God forbid, an idiot? Indeed, this scouting expedition was the direct result of the alarms sounding Marcus' mind as he had listened a few days ago to Lady Monteagle. From what he could gather—and he dared not ask a direct question of her lest she blast him where he stood—she had all but made the match on his behalf.

Bearing in mind the advanced age of the lady, and her connection with his cousin Geoffrey, Marcus could not but deal politely with her. Too bad Geoffrey's wish had come true: Lady Monteagle had indeed found someone else to harry!

At least Marcus could, quite simply, neglect to call on the Foresters when they came to town. But yet—suppose she was as intelligent, amiable, delightful, as reported?

He would soon know.

From distant reaches of the house came small scurrying noises, and Marcus counseled himself to be patient. With wry humor he decided that this day must be the footman's first day on duty, for he did not even escort the visitor to a reception room.

Marcus now had not the slightest doubt: he was the world's fool to come, and his heart beat loudly in the region of his well-polished boots, where it had unaccountably sunk. Perhaps a king might carry off such an expedition to view a prospective mate, but not Marcus!

Left to cool his heels for perhaps five minutes—a period that seemed much longer—he advanced tentatively into the hall. A fine spacious staircase in the grand manner of an earlier day rose directly from the hall into the upper floors. Marcus turned his back on it so as not to seem to be searching the private areas of the house.

He turned away just a moment too soon.

Lottie's bedroom, in which she had recently spent

what her mother considered to be an excessive amount
of time, faced the east lawn. Developments at the front
of the south-facing house were hidden from her view.
Thus she was not aware of the arrival of the visitor.

So Lottie, unsuspecting that Lady Monteagle's
candidate for her future stood in the foyer below, came
tripping down the hall to the head of the stairs. Over the
banister she caught sight of her mother descending the
curving stairway, obviously on her way to greet the
visitor she now saw standing, still in his driving coat, in
the hall below. The man had his back to her. In a
moment he would turn.

But before that moment, Lottie heard the fateful
words.

"Mr. North?" her mother greeted the stranger.
"Welcome to Pentstable!"

Lottie gasped. Her mother had betrayed her!

Her mother had actually invited the man here to
Pentstable in an outrageous bid to force Lottie's hand.
If Lottie refused to see him in London, as she had deter-
mined to do, then she would perforce see him at
Pentstable!

No other explanation could be possible. In fact, no
other even occurred to her. The notion that a man might
journey down from London solely to meet her, even
though vouched for by Lady Forester's friend, was not
one Lottie could entertain for a moment.

Well, then! Lottie knew that if she acquiesced in this
simple thing—to meet a man she had told her mother
she would not meet—then her mother could, inch by
inch, move Lottie closer to marriage until, still without
knowing quite how she had arrived there, she might well
stand at the altar with a man she did not even like.

There was a way out, of course. Flight—her only
chance. And she must take it.

She clutched the banister to steady herself, and
looked down, hoping that, being merely a dream, he

would vanish. He did not. His figure was foreshortened in her view, making him look excessively short and broad. In fact, he was of stocky build, with powerful and broad shoulders. His hair was dark brown, thick and springy, as though possessed of a life of its own.

She stood as though paralyzed, taking in every aspect of this strange man with whose future she might have been involved. He was not repulsive, at least from this distance, but she would never lessen the distance between them, never!

Tyson scurried in through the baize door from the kitchens, clearly having just put off his apron and donned his black coat. As the newcomer bent forward to give his caped coat to the butler, she noticed a little dark curl at the nape of his neck. Lottie swallowed. The curl was surprisingly disarming, and could even, in other circumstances, seem beguiling.

He moved, as though he could feel the touch of her intense gaze on his back. Suddenly the danger of discovery in which she stood occurred to her, and she turned in panic, lifted her skirts, and fled silently back to her room.

The next half-hour was a busy time for her. Her cloak was providentially close at hand and she donned it. Pulling her bandbox from the wardrobe, she realized that, with only the vaguest forethought, she was about to take a fateful step, the outcome of which she could not know.

To get out of the house and get to the village inn in time for the stagecoach, to find dear Miss Wythe's cottage in Alford, and not to be caught on the way . . .

· A sense of foreboding touched her. Would she ever come again to this house, sleep in this room? Then she remembered that she had eaten very little for breakfast, and it was most likely hunger that directed her thoughts. Perhaps she could get something to eat at the inn, although she shuddered at the prospect of old Ben's

searching questions as to why she was taking the coach
—and unaccompanied at that.

Nonetheless, flight was indicated, flight had been
carefully planned, and flight would take place. She
eased out of her bedroom. She closed and, after a
moment's hesitation, locked the door behind her. She
would gain precious time if the servants had to break
down the door before finding her gone. She hurried to
the back stairs.

She found she had not needed to fear any interference
by the servants. To a man, and woman, every one was
positioned by the baize door to the front hall, anxious to
get a good look at the stranger. They had no doubt that
he had come to offer for Miss Lottie. Snippets of over-
heard discussions between Lady Forester and her
daughter had been pieced together to make a seamless
fabric. Miss Lottie was about to be wed!

She was out of the house, and well on her way along
the lane leading to the village, before the curiosity
rampant in the servants' hall was satisfied. Opinion was
divided. Nettie the frivolous thought he was not near
handsome enough for Miss Lottie.

"Miss Lottie herself ain't all that handsome herself,"
said Connors, the parlormaid, "which is not to say she's
not nice, but after all, it's Miss Carrie who'll sweep the
beaux of London off their feet."

Nettie stood up for her opinions. "But if I was a man
looking for a wife, I'd not take Miss Carrie. That one!
Selfish as the day is long. And cruel with it."

Mrs. Tyson, the cook, who had been in the Forester
household since Lady Forester had come to live there on
her marriage, said grudgingly, "It's not fit to talk about
them. But that white streak in Miss Lottie's hair can't be
just wiped away. Miss Carrie did that, hit her with a
horseshoe she picked up in the stable in some quarrel
they had, and the hair never grew back right. It was
hushed up, but mark my words, Miss Carrie was doing

something she shouldn't ha' been, and never a word of I'm sorry until her mother made her. Not that that helped Miss Lottie's hair much.''

Nettie leaned forward, ready to hear more from the usually taciturn cook, but the arrival of Tyson, bearing instructions for refreshments to be served at once in the salon, put an end to the instructive little gossip.

In the meantime, in the salon, Lady Forester was exerting herself to make the unexpected visitor feel at home. She had sent word to Lottie that her presence as eldest daughter was requested in the salon.

Refreshments had been served, and still Lottie did not appear.

Lady Forester had questioned Mr. North about his journey from London—"very comfortable." She asked how he had left London; the answer came: "Crowded, but of course one expects that."

What one did *not* expect, Marcus reflected, was that it would take such a long time for the daughter of the house to appear in answer to her mother's summons. His curiosity grew. Drinking the last swallow of his third dish of tea, he looked again at the door. Still no Miss Forester. He discerned that Lady Forester herself was rapidly losing her temper.

To his dismay, he was gradually becoming aware that the tables were turned. He had come on an impulse, rather *de haut en bas*, to examine the young lady who was willing—nay, eager, according to Lady Monteagle —to receive him, and in all probability, again according to Lady Monteagle, to accept an offer of marriage in due course.

Now, not only was the heiress not quivering with anticipation at the prospect of seeing him, but it was apparent from her bewildered manner that Lady Forester herself was at sea over the purpose of his visit. Clearly Lady Monteagle had exaggerated the Forester response to making the acquaintance of Marcus North.

Geoffrey's mother-in-law had made a fool of him, so much seemed certain.

He longed for the earth to open up and swallow him whole. Failing that, his main wish now was to make his excuses and depart. But Lady Forester, at last realizing that the man Fenella Monteagle had said might be captured for Lottie had come for the sole purpose of meeting her daughter, had no mind to let him go, now that he was here.

She rang the bell for Tyson. He came in at once, as though he had been hovering outside the door for some time. Yet Marcus thought he seemed out of breath, and even a bit wild-eyed, as though faced with circumstances he did not know how to control.

"Miss Forester," said her mother, a chill in her voice, "is descending soon?"

Tyson took a deep breath. "Miss Forester sends her apologies," he said, "but she is not feeling well, and asks to be excused."

"Not well!" exclaimed Lady Forester. "She was fine at breakfast!" Too late she realized her indiscretion. "But of course," she amended without truth, "I thought she looked pale." She turned to Marcus. "I cannot tell you how sorry I am that my daughter must be excused. You know how missish young girls can be. Only a momentary touch of the vapors, I am sure of it . . ."

Babbling on, she gave Marcus an impression completely opposite from the one she was attempting. Marcus felt a strong bond of sympathy with the unknown Miss Forester.

He realized he had begun for the first time to think of a wife as a person with thoughts of her own, wishes that she set store by, in fact to believe her to be an individual. As—he told himself—Annabella was not. He needed time to think about this revelation, but on the whole he rather believed he favored it.

He was invited to return the next day, when the young lady would feel more the thing. Surrounded by Lady Forester's apologies as though by a cloud of gnats, he made his escape and drove down the drive on his way to the village, where he hoped to find rooms for the night.

Behind him, at Pentstable, the household was in a state of mind resembling panic. "Now then, Tyson," said Lady Forester in an icy rage, "what is this about Miss Lottie being ill? I vow that girl is no more ill than I am!"

Without waiting for an answer, she strode to the stairs and began to ascend. Before she reached the third step, she was aware of Tyson's cough, a sound designed to arrest the hearer in her tracks.

"Begging pardon, my lady," he said, "but Miss Lottie is not in her room."

"Not in her room? How do you know that?"

"We . . . we went in. Thinking she was ill, you might say." Although he was stung by the active disbelief he saw in his mistress's expression, he did not see fit to add that he and Nellie had been required to pick the lock to gain entry.

Able to speak at last, Lady Forester inquired, "And she was not in her room?"

"To be precise, my lady, she is not in the house."

Lady Forester descended to the lobby floor. "Not in the house," she repeated. "Then, Tyson, will you be so good as to stop this . . . this equivocation and tell me precisely where she is?"

Miserably the butler answered, "I do not know."

The tale was soon told. The servants had, while Lady Forester and the visitor sat in idle conversation in the salon, searched the house, and even the grounds immediately surrounding the house, without success.

"The truth is," Tyson said finally, "that Miss Lottie has disappeared."

Lady Forester was stunned. She had, of course,

informed Lottie that the girl would indeed receive Mr. North in London. Lottie's protests she had ignored. Now it was clear the girl was definitely and outrageously rebellious. Lottie did not intend to meet Mr. North *anywhere*.

When Lottie returned, Lady Forester would have a few choice and persuasive words to say to her!

She became aware of her butler watching her anxiously. She pulled herself together.

"Well, Tyson, if you have searched the house, then I must accept that she is not here. But 'disappeared' is, I think, much too strong a word to use. Miss Lottie has only gone for a stroll, and was tempted to walk beyond the park. We shall see her for supper, I am sure."

Tyson, however, was not as certain. He knew what he had seen when Nettie and he had gone into Miss Lottie's room, expecting to find its occupant unconscious on the floor. It was no simple stroll in the park which required a bandbox, an extra pair of slippers, nightwear, and a few gowns, modest in style but of quality. It was clear to Nettie, and to the other servants when apprised of the news, that Miss Lottie would not be home for supper.

But, as Lady Forester's servants had learned, it was not always wise to offer unasked-for information.

5

MARCUS NORTH, reaching the village inn an hour after the coach to Alford had departed, carrying away the object of Marcus' honorable intentions, had much to think about. He was given a comfortable bed, soft and well-aired, and the food was passable. He had had much worse fare on the Continent. In truth, several meals in Germany he remembered vividly as having been spurned by the local dogs.

He had not intended to stay in this vicinity. He had planned to go to Pentstable, make his surveillance under the guise of civility, bearing messages from Lady Monteagle, and then decide whether to return to London and pursue Miss Forester or to retreat to the fastness of Gresham.

Now, however, Marcus sat in a private sitting room nursing some surprisingly good brandy—smuggled in from France, without a doubt—and considered the day's developments. He was no fool. If Lady Forester did not know today that her daughter was ill—and surely her surprise could not have been feigned—then she could have no assurance that the young lady would be recovered tomorrow.

Only his strong sense of duty required him to call again at Pentstable on the morrow. The situation now, to his mind, seemed to stretch beyond the limits of "awkward," all the way to "disastrous."

"Awkward" was not the word currently in use at Pentstable. Lottie did not return, as expected by her mother, as soon as Marcus was out of sight. At length Carrie, while never in her sister's confidence, had, by a judicious use of threats, induced Nettie to unburden her conscience. It was a matter of moments thereafter that Lady Forester learned the extent of Lottie's defection, as signified by the missing garments.

"I won't believe it! That my child could be so deceitful! Stealing away," continued Lady Forester, her anger running deep, "without so much as a word to me! Not that I should have allowed her to leave the house. Lady Monteagle has clearly read Mr. North aright and he is seeking a wife. Why should he not choose Lottie? But she has given him a very regrettable impression of her. And how she can expect to repair this damage, I cannot think."

"Mama," Amanda interrupted shyly, "Lottie did say she didn't want to even meet him."

"Of course she did!" Lady Forester rounded on her youngest daughter. "That's what all well-brought-up young ladies say at first. Mind you remember that, Amanda, and you too, Carrie. But how was I to know she meant it?" After a moment Lady Forester continued in a more moderate vein. "She didn't mean it, that is all. She simply shied at the thought of meeting the man face-to-face. Although I do feel his coming uninvited was not quite the thing. Well, she'll be back by teatime."

Lottie did not return by teatime. By late afternoon it was learned that she had not taken her mare, Cooper, for an extended ride, nor had she, even though she was the whip of the family—her father disdaining even to try to teach his other daughters the rudiments of driving—taken the phaeton. That was the most remote possibility, for where would she drive? The neighbors were well-acquainted with the Foresters, and certainly there would be talk were Lottie to appear alone at their door. Surely the girl was too proud to seek shelter with them.

Lady Forester's anger, quite naturally, subsided in due course, and transformed itself into a real anxiety for the girl's safety. Surely if there had been an accident she would have been notified. Throughout the long night watches, she returned again and again to the embarrassment that Lottie forced on her, and she truly did not know what she would say to Mr. North on the morrow.

In the end, she had no need to say overmuch the next day to Lottie's would-be suitor. Nothing could gloss over the bald fact that Lottie was not receiving company, at least at Pentstable. However, Lady Forester managed to give the firm impression that her daughter was absent only for the day, because she was too shy to be introduced to him.

How they would go on, after they were wed—if he did fancy her—he could not conjecture. A lifetime of bedroom doors locked against him had no allure at all, no matter how intelligent and well-read she might be. To say nothing, he added, of the amiable disposition Lady Monteagle had given her credit for.

His manners, he hoped later, had served him well, for he was out of the house and into his curricle without knowing quite what he said or how he had taken his leave. Irving, being without instructions, drove to the inn where he had stayed overnight, expecting to pay his call on Miss Forester this morning. Well, he had paid his call, for what that was worth, and now there was no place to go but to Gresham Manor. He was about to give instructions to that effect, when suddenly he could not face the long journey into the north, to be met at the end by a lonely house.

"We'll return to London," he instructed his coachman. Lights, music, ladies who at least did not disappear before they had even met him! And when the

Foresters arrived in town, then he might find Gresham appealing.

A fortnight in London only etched the situation more deeply in his mind. He went through the motions of social intercourse as before, but this time he was aware of another, completely different level of thought carrying on in its own way as an undercurrent to his days and nights among the *ton*.

On this secret level, a few things became plain to him. One was that, among other things, he had lost Pomfret Priory. But strangely, that loss was as nothing compared with the loss of a dream he had not known he had. Pomfret would have been a pleasant addition to his own holdings, rounding out the western border nicely. But in the long run, Gresham was ample for his needs, and he was not a greedy man.

But, although he would have denied that he was in any way fanciful, something deeper in his masculine self was stirring, forcing its way to the surface of his mind. In between dances at Devonshire House, between bouts at Jackson's Gym, and in the small hours of the night in his lonely rooms, he began to see what he had lost.

No, the dream that came to him with some force, as though it had lain hidden for a long time, was that one day a lady of quality, one of the ladies perhaps across the room at Almack's, or standing at the right hand of Lady Jersey in a receiving line, a lady, at any rate, would accept him, square and unprepossessing as he believed himself, prosy and too conventional, and would see in him something of value to her.

The years ahead, a growing family, a settled contentment at Gresham Manor, with a kindly lady at his side —this was the dream he had not known was so strong in him.

Insistent now in his mind, the dream could only remind him that the first lady of quality he had ever seriously considered—for he had little real intention of taking Annabella to wive—had fled the country before she even *saw* him!

In spite of all its gaiety, London was ashes on the tongue. From a distance, Gresham Manor, even solitary as it was, possessed an alluring aura of green trees and lawn, cooling breezes carrying the freshness of flowering things, and, although he would not have used the words, a healing balm in the comforting embrace of his own house.

In a fortnight he had wound up his affairs in London, had bidden farewell to Geoffrey—but not to Lady Monteagle—had instructed his servants to pack and return home, and, with only his groom, had set out in his curricle on the Great North Road toward Gresham Manor.

While Marcus, two weeks earlier, still sat in the drawing room at Pentstable, Lottie gained the coaching inn before she was missed by her family. She had an idea of the tumult that was bound to erupt upon the discovery that she was not there to meet her intended betrothed. But she also had a fair idea of the depth of her mother's distress.

Lottie out in the world without family support or knowledge would take second place to Lottie defiantly refusing to marry a perfect stranger. In this she did her mother an injustice, although she did not know it.

Lottie believed the servants would take her part, as much as they could. They certainly would cover up her absence until it was required to say truth. In this, she was accurate. Even though she had not taken any into her confidence, she knew that the servants had seen the years of her mother's bullying, and her mother's clear indulgence of Caroline, and had not approved.

There was often an extra hot brick in her bed on

winter nights, and a special trip up the back stairs with a
nightcap of hot chocolate. Lottie knew that her mother
and sisters had no such amenities given without asking.

So when Lottie alighted from the coach in Alford, her
tightly packed bandbox in her hand, she was filled with
good humor and a certain self-congratulation that all
her plans had gone well.

She had escaped that man, she gauged that a fortnight
away from home would give tempers a chance to
subside, and in the meantime she would enjoy that fortnight with her dear Miss Wythe, perhaps the only true
friend she had in the world.

Miss Wythe was, as Lottie had expected, delighted to
see her. Her features, upon seeing Lottie on the door-
step, radiated delight and warm affection—at first.

"My dear Lottie! What a surprise! Do come in." She
looked over Lottie's shoulder, clearly expecting to see
Lady Forester. "Well, no matter," she said cryptically.
"You will tell me in due course. But first, a cup of tea.
You have just now come from Pentstable? But don't tell
me yet. I . . . I think I need the restorative as much as
you."

Miss Wythe turned toward the back of her little
cottage. This was not the first time Lottie had visited
her, of course, but for the first time since she had left
Pentstable that morning she began to have doubts as to
her wisdom in coming.

The cottage was smaller than she remembered. Sitting
now in a chintz-covered chair, and looking around her
with the eyes of one who expected to become a member
of the household, however temporarily, she realized
that there was no spare bedroom. There was little room
to spare in the sitting room—if she stretched out her feet
to ease her cramped knees, she could touch another
chair on her right, and a table on her left.

Well, she had intended all along to return to

Pentstable in another fortnight, so she would simply alter her plans. A few days here, and then she would return to brave the dying embers of her mother's fury.

Tea had been drunk, and little cakes had been eaten, when Lottie put words to the vague uneasiness she had felt. Miss Wythe's hand shook when she set her cup down. A weary look in her eyes, and shadows beneath them . . .

"Dear Miss Wythe, please tell me what's wrong."

"My dear . . . there's nothing . . ." The governess met Lottie's eyes and decided to tell the truth. "It is only a trifle, after all."

"A trifle that keeps you from sleeping? I think not." A chilling thought struck her. "Miss Wythe, have you seen a doctor?"

"Yes, I have. And that's the trouble!" Miss Wythe's words came out in a rush.

There was no time for delicate questioning. "What did he say?"

"My dear Lottie, don't look like that! Please! He said there is nothing serious wrong with me. I have this terrible pain in my leg sometimes and he has given me medicine for it. It makes me so *drowsy*! I think it must be some kind of opium!" She laughed shortly. "Do you think dear Lady Forester will suspect you have come to stay in an Oriental harem?"

"No, she won't," said Lottie, so briskly that her former mentor, knowing her well, gave vent to her suspicions.

"Your mother does know you are here, does she not?"

"To put it quite bluntly, no, dear Miss Wythe, she does not."

Miss Wythe leaned back in her chair and contemplated her visitor with an impassive gaze. The girl was in trouble, that was sure, and she must be helped. But Miss Wythe was also caught in the toils of her own dilemma. However, first things, she knew, came first.

"Tell me."

It was such a relief, thought Lottie, to unburden herself of all the distress of the past days to a listener who did not interrupt, who did not frown, and who did not hold out the promise of retribution to come.

Miss Wythe listened carefully, and if she were outraged by the unconventional arrangement by Lady Forester to bring the second daughter into society before Lottie, one could not have discerned it from the governess's features. Moreover, and this was more to the point, she did not allow any criticism of her beloved former charge, now confessing her unseemly unchaperoned flight from her home, to appear either.

She had known well enough that Lottie was not favored by her mother, and received treatment that, to Miss Wythe's eye, bordered on cruelty.

But now, when Lottie's voice had at last trailed away, Miss Wythe could not hide her very real apprehension over the possible consequences of Lottie's rash flight.

"You think I was wrong," Lottie accused her. "Tell me the worst."

"The worst that can happen, I suppose," said the older lady thoughtfully, "is that Mr.—North, is it?—will return to London—"

"Which I devoutly hope he has already done!"

"—and your mother," continued Miss Wythe, ignoring Lottie's interruption, "will take your defiance very much amiss."

"In fact, she will never let me forget it."

And, thought Lottie, I'll be confined to Pentstable for the rest of my life! While her own funds were adequate for her needs, yet to set up a separate establishment, renting a house for example in Bath and staffing it with servants, maintaining a coach and horses—that was beyond her means.

Except, of course, for Pomfret Priory. She might sell it and spend the money—or of course she had every right to remove to the Priory herself, and live there. Only a week ago she had considered this possibility and decided that Pomfret was too far away from any social activities, and that she might as well resign from the world, the way unwanted Plantagenet women were said to have done, founding convents and living in retirement.

A week ago such a fate had seemed dreadful to her. Now, recognizing her likely future with clear sight borrowed from Miss Wythe, she could foresee that life at Pentstable would be no more alluring than her remote life at Pomfret promised to be.

She sighed deeply. She was too tired to think clearly, she decided. A quick look at her hostess revealed a gray, drawn expression that told of Miss Wythe's pain even more than fatigue.

"Dear Miss Wythe!" said Lottie, overcome by the sharp sting of conscience. "I should never have troubled you with my small upsets. I am persuaded you are too ill for me to impose my presence on you. I should have seen at once that my arrival was untimely. I shall find a room at the inn—unless I can help? Pray tell me what I can do for you."

Miss Wythe smiled. "It is true that this foolish ailment does take up much of my attention. But I promise you it is better than last week. You are no trouble at all, and I shall not hear of your removing to an inn room. Without an abigail? Your mother would never forgive me!"

"She would not have to know . . ." began Lottie, but abandoned her protest at once, hearing how feeble it sounded. "I should never have come!"

"No, you are wrong, Lottie. It is possible—indeed

quite probable—that your coming to me was guided by providence."

"How can that be?"

"My dear, I shall want to think a bit more on this. In the meantime, if you could help me prepare our light supper, I shall be grateful."

Lottie's night was far from untroubled. There was little room in Miss Wythe's cottage for an overnight guest. Indeed, Lottie felt a pang of guilt that she had never expressed an interest in her governess's situation in her frequent letters. It now seemed to Lottie that she had written only of her own affairs, confiding in Miss Wythe as she had been wont to do when her governess was still at Pentstable.

Never, she now realized, had she inquired as to whether Miss Wythe were happy in her Alford home: did she want for any comfort, or did her health continue to be good?

She knew herself to be as selfish as Caroline, although in a greatly different way. Cosseted to a degree, Carrie craved even more attention. Lottie too, although all but ignored at home, unburdened herself to Miss Wythe.

The night wore on. From her makeshift bed, consisting of a pair of chairs arranged as comfortably as possible, Lottie heard Miss Wythe turn in her sleep and utter a slight groan at the pain in her leg as she changed position. She might assure Lottie that her leg was much better and that the doctor had told her a cure would come in good time, but the pain persisted now, and it seemed to be severe.

What could Lottie do for her? Not much. Even her presence in the tiny house was distressing, although her hostess would not admit it. Lottie must either go on the morrow—which was already here, she realized, seeing a faint light at the windows—back to Pentstable, or, taking an irrevocable step in her life, go on north to Pomfret.

It was not a decision to make hastily, and on that note she fell asleep at last.

In the end, she was spared that decision.

Instead, the alternative presented to her was one she could not even have dreamed of.

"My dear," began Miss Wythe after breakfast was finished and the small kitchen made clean, "I suppose you will return soon to Pentstable?"

"I am not certain."

"Please believe that you are welcome here, as though you were my own daughter. But you do not see any other choice, do you?"

Slowly Lottie said, "Do you know, I have been thinking very favorably of Pomfret." At her mentor's uncomprehending expression, she added, "You remember Pomfret Priory was willed to me by my Grandmother Forester? It was her home when she was a girl."

"I remember her well. Lottie, you are so much like her! A woman of character, and well-connected. Adelia Granville had her choice of suitors, so I have heard."

"But Mama says she was plain, and so am I."

"I should not like to say your mama was wrong, because it is not my place to judge her. But believe me when I say that Adelia Granville was courted by many a beau, and not for her fortune, either, which, after all, was not enormous." Miss Wythe sighed. "No one ever understood."

"Why she married my grandfather? I did not know him."

"Nor did I. But I have heard much. Now, my child, do you really think you might go north to Pomfret? Have you really considered making such a drastic change in your life?"

"I just don't know! One moment I think I should go home, to take whatever punishment Mama decides upon . . ."

Even though Lottie is nineteen, thought Miss Wythe, she will accept punishment as though she were only nine! Lady Forester had much to answer for, in the governess's opinion.

"And the next moment I long to be at Pomfret, my own mistress for once. Although," she commented wryly, "I suppose my Granville cousin who lives there now will conceive it her duty to give me her advice!"

They sat in companionable silence for a bit. Miss Wythe wondered whether she dared broach the scheme that had come to her as she had listened to Lottie's narrative the afternoon before. It had indeed seemed like the intervention of providence, but impulse was often misleading, and she had decided to sleep on it. Now the plan, while seeming bright and alluring yesterday, shimmered in uncertainty.

But faint heart never reached certainty, she told herself, and she decided to take the risk.

"The problem, Lottie, is not my leg, painful though that may be. The doctor assures me that rest and medicine will effect a cure, and I shall be as good as new in perhaps three months."

"If you'll be well again, then what difficulty can there be?"

"Quite simply, it is this . . ."

Miss Wythe had accepted a position as governess in a family whose home lay a day's journey to the north of Alford. Her charge would be the five-year-old daughter of the house, who was said to be an invalid.

"A manor in the country, and only one female to teach—it sounded ideal. I did wonder, of course, whether I would find the family congenial, since the father, who is now dead, I believe, was in trade, and received his title for some obscure reason. It is most likely that he quite simply purchased it. But if the girl is an invalid, I expected not to consort with Lady Drysdale at all, but to spend my time with the child.''

Lottie paid close attention. "But you say *expected*, as though this opportunity has passed."

"Well, most likely it has. I cannot ride a day's journey, nor can I climb to a nursery room, nor . . . In short, my dear, I must refuse the position."

"I'm sorry."

"The trouble is that I have already accepted it. Now Lady Drysdale will believe I do not keep my word, and I fear she may ruin my reputation. I suggested she write to your mother and to two other ladies who I believed would give her a good report of my abilities and character. If she complains to them that I failed to keep my agreement with her, then—"

Miss Wythe stopped short, and Lottie was dismayed to see tears starting in the older lady's eyes. "But surely she cannot blame you if you are too ill to take up the position?"

"I do not know the lady. But I did make inquiries about the family, of course. The Drysdales have no breeding, and I fear the worst."

Miss Wythe waited for Lottie's comment. She had promised herself that she would explain her dilemma to the girl, but not take her thought a step further. She hoped—goodness, how she hoped!—that Lottie might find it possible to take up the position for her. Certainly a Miss Forester might be preferred over a mere Miss Wythe, since Miss Forester's connections were impeccable if not lofty.

The Drysdale position would give Lottie time enough to decide what she wished to do, return to Pentstable or move on to Pomfret. Besides, thought Miss Wythe practically, Lottie would likely find out that being a governess had serious drawbacks, and might well decide to return to Pentstable, make her peace with her mother, marry Mr. North if he were still available, and live happily ever after.

But Lottie saw the impersonation as a great lark—one, moreover, which would put her farther out of her mother's disciplinary reach. She smiled brightly.

"When do I start?"

6

L OTTIE HAD been in the Drysdale ménage for less
than a sennight when she recognized that, had she
known the whole of the situation, she might well have
returned in haste to the haven of Pentstable.

Although she knew Miss Wythe to be in the ordinary
way a woman of transparent honesty, Lottie realized
that, either her former governess had been misinformed
as to the nature of the proposed employment, or Miss
Wythe herself, harried by the demands of her livelihood
and financial future, had conveniently glossed over
certain aspects of the position under discussion.

While the atmosphere in her own home had been
heated by bickering and unwelcome pressure on her to
show off her paces, like a show pony on the block at
Tattersall's, at this point Lottie believed she could cope
with that harassment more competently than she could
deal with one really very nice five-year-old invalid and
her mother.

When Lottie first arrived, her interview with Lady
Drysdale was uneventful. Lottie's main purpose was to
remember to answer to the name Miss Wythe without a
telltale hesitation, and much that Lady Drysdale told
her failed to engage her attention. The simple elements
of the situation were buried in a rambling monologue to
which Lottie responded civilly.

She learned that Delia, frail from birth, occupied a
suite of rooms at the top of the house, from which she
rarely emerged. Lottie, in the guise of Miss Wythe,

would be introduced to the child by Mrs. Linn, the housekeeper.

"My nerves cannot abide seeing my child in such dire straits," Lady Drysdale told Lottie. "I am sure my distress must upset the dear girl, and I do try to keep her best interests at heart, you know."

"I am sure you do," murmured the new governess politely. Lady Drysdale surely could not mean, thought Lottie, that she did not visit the child? What a lonely existence that must be! Lottie began to wonder what the girl must look like, if her own mother could not bear to see her.

Lottie's imagination ran riot. At least at Pentstable one did not feel neglected by one's mama. In fact, the situation there was quite the opposite. Lottie recalled more than one occasion when her own best interests would have been well-served by a little benign neglect on the part of her mama—such as in the matter of her proposed marriage. But all that was behind her now. She was "Miss Wythe," gainfully employed, and marriage was far from her mind. She would recall that thought very soon, and the irony of it would escape her.

"Delia—that is short for Cordelia, you know . . . my late husband, Lord Drysdale, was a great admirer of the Bard. He believed he had a particular affinity for King Lear. Although, of course, he had only the one son, before Delia was born."

Lottie must have looked her bewilderment. How could a man with one son be compared with a king who had three daughters? Lady Drysdale provided, unasked, the answer. "I have not read the play myself, of course, nor have I seen it on the stage. I find that reading gives me the headache. But my dear husband did repeat a word or two from time to time. Something about a serpent's tooth? Perhaps you know the phrase. I cannot think why he should have tormented me so—he knew that I cannot abide reptiles of any description."

A thankless child, then. Lottie began to wonder what kind of monster might be contained in a frail five-year-old girl. The question in her mind was answered in Lady Drysdale's next breath.

"Of course you will meet my stepson, Sir Albin." Lady Drysdale's voice faltered. "I had not expected him to be at home, you know, when I wrote to you at the first. He will insist upon interviewing you, although what he knows about governesses I cannot think. But . . ."

Lady Drysdale was slender to the point of angularity, and now for the first time Lottie could discern a shakiness in her hands. Surely that tremor had come only with the mention of her stepson! And if there be monsters here, thought Lottie with a regrettable lack of gravity, then she believed she had just now been presented with his name.

"Sir Albin?" Lottie murmured. "But I did not expect—"

"Of course you didn't," interrupted Lady Drysdale, suddenly cross. "No one did. He's come rushing from London only last week for no reason that he chooses to tell me, although I cannot help but think that the details of his latest scrape may not suit delicate ears."

A tenor voice, rather pleasing, interrupted them, and they both turned toward the door. There stood a man dressed in top boots and tan country clothes, with an air of what Lottie could only deem a well-nurtured conviction of his manifest superiority to his fellows. Lottie took a dislike to him on sight.

Later, she realized her instant reaction to him was caused by the way his hot eyes assessed her in mere seconds, from her primly dressed hair to her booted toes, and gave her the clear impression that she had failed to measure up to his standards, whatever they might be. Inwardly she shuddered.

Surely she would not lose her job—or rather Miss

Wythe's job—before she even had a chance to meet her prospective charge! But Lottie had not thoroughly taken on the protective coloring of Miss Wythe's submissive nature. She was only temporarily a governess. At base, she was still Miss Forester of Pentstable. She eyed the intruder levelly while Lady Drysdale made incoherent introductions.

"Then," said Sir Albin, with an edge to his voice, "you are to form part of my household? I confess, dear Mama"—his voice when he spoke to his stepmother was cruelly sarcastic—"I should like to be informed before such an appointment is made. Whatever happened to the old witch my dear sister had before? Did Delia put her to rout too?"

Unjustly accused, Lady Drysdale was moved to protest. "You know very well that you were not here to be consulted until last week, and I had already engaged Miss Wythe! And I think, really, Albin, that the choice of a governess for my daughter is far better left to me."

"You spoil the child," he said bluntly. "She's no more an invalid than I am."

Lady Drysdale made a small gesture of denial, but clearly, decided Lottie, the woman was afraid of her stepson. However, Lottie was not, at least at the moment. She was far more fearful of doing Miss Wythe's reputation a mischief than she was of this over-grown lout. She did not recognize her mistake yet.

She stood sturdily, in what she belatedly hoped was the posture of a governess rather than that of a well-bred young lady, particularly one who was possessed of a reasonable property. Even if her person were not attractive, her ownership of Pomfret Priory apparently was, to Mr. North, and she realized to her great surprise that that offer of marriage had given her enough confidence to stiffen her spine now. She was plain, she was intelligently educated, and she could have been at this very moment planning her wedding to a gentleman of substance. If she felt a twinge of regret at what she had rejected, she ignored it.

But Sir Albin Drysdale was not sensitive enough to assess her correctly. What he saw was a mousily dressed governess of the kind he had nothing but contempt for. His philosophy, due to being given too much wealth too soon, held that women were enamored of his person, and were more than willing to accept what portion of his attention he chose to bestow on them. He had so far not met anyone who did not agree with this tenet of his faith. He had in fact come to view all women, including his stepmother and his half-sister, and now most likely the latest in a series of governesses, with unveiled contempt.

Subtly Lottie became aware of his opinion, and felt a flush rise warmly from her neck into her cheeks. A sharp word or two hesitated on the tip of her tongue, designed and ready to put this upstart in his place, but in time she remembered she was Miss Wythe, and the words died before they could be spoken.

"I suppose," Sir Albin said to his stepmother, looking past Lottie as though she were not visible, "that this one will last no longer than the previous one. It's immaterial to me whom you engage." So saying, he turned on his well-booted heel and left.

To Lottie's surprise, Lady Drysdale seemed more distressed than the occasion warranted. It was clear that her stepson was an obnoxious bully, but why should she cringe so? Surely he would not offer violence to his father's widow? Unless, of course, Lady Drysdale's money was in his hands. How helpless a lady was without a source of funds all her own! But Lady Drysdale did not explain. Instead, she indicated that the interview was finished.

"Pray pull that bell," she requested of Lottie, and, when the butler appeared, added, "Penn, ask Mrs. Linn to conduct Miss Wythe upstairs to Miss Delia. Miss

Wythe will have the room next to Miss Delia's. I am sure you will take care of her.''

Lottie did not have time to do more than notice that last odd remark of her employer's.

Mrs. Linn was a stout, pleasant-faced woman who puffed up the stairs from the foyer to the bedroom floor, and then down a long hall to a stairway that climbed to an upper floor.

''Lady Drysdale wanted Miss Delia not to be disturbed by the noises of the household,'' she explained to Lottie. ''From an infant she was puny, and cried so that the master—old Sir Richard, I mean—couldn't stand it. That's really why she was put at the top of the house. And after the master died, it just seemed more . . . more suitable.''

''The house does not seem unduly noisy,'' murmured Lottie. In truth, she was wondering whether she and the housekeeper were the only folk in the house, beyond the butler and the two Drysdales. She was conscious of a quiet that seemed almost unnatural. She shook herself mentally. Miss Wythe would have scorned such fantasies, and so must Lottie. She was here to accomplish a good deed for her loved governess, to save her reputation, to save her job.

But what would happen when Miss Wythe recovered? Lottie could not stay here forever as a governess. She had a family to which to return, or—supposing Marcus North still lingered in the wings—her own property to resort to. Not that Pomfret Priory held any allure save as a haven from storm, but it was hers, an asylum for the harried.

Just now, her situation would be at least comfortable. Lady Drysdale might well demand reports on her daughter's progress, but it seemed likely that she would not be an interfering visitor in the schoolroom! And certainly Miss Wythe could not come to take up the position in her own person—not when the Drysdales believed that "Miss Wythe" was a slender, boyish young lady with enormous green eyes and a white streak in her light auburn hair!

Well, she could not worry about that yet. Her immediate duties would take up all her time.

Young Miss Cordelia Drysdale was small for her age. She had a wealth of flaxen hair, dressed—so Lottie learned—by Parsons, Lady Drysdale's own maid, a circumstance that explained the very mature style that made the child appear at first to be a dwarfed old woman staring fearfully at her visitors.

"Here's your new governess, my dear," cried Mrs. Linn with aggressive cheerfulness. "I told you you'd have company before long. Trust your mama for that!"

Delia's great eyes were fixed on Lottie. The girl was sitting in a chair drawn up to a roaring fire in the grate, looking for a moment—a very frightened moment for Lottie—like a kind of misshapen furry monster.

Suddenly the mound of fur that had seemed to be an ugly growth on the child erupted in a spasm of wild barking and launched itself at Lottie.

Several things happened at once: Lottie's heart stopped for a measurable space of time, Delia cried out, "Puff!" and Mrs. Linn deftly caught the small furry missile.

"Now then, Puff! Shame on you! Quit your wiggling or you won't get any more little sugar tarts, I'll see to that. Now, look for yourself. Miss Wythe is a nice lady, Delia, I'll thank you to say something to this beast to teach him Christian behavior."

Delia joined the spirited discussion in which the small dog was a speechless, but not silent, participant, and at length quiet was restored.

"I'll leave you to get acquainted," said Mrs. Linn comfortably. "Miss Wythe, I expect you'll want your meals up here with Miss Delia, but if you want, come down to the kitchen. You'll be welcome in the hall any-time."

When she was gone, Lottie turned to Delia. "Which would you like, to have me stay or go down to the hall?" She thought a moment and added, "I suppose it's too soon to ask that."

"You'll like it better up here," said Delia in a matter-of-fact way. "Of course she means the servants' hall, you know. Mama will not want you to eat with the family." Surprisingly, she added, "I don't think you'd like it, either."

Lottie, at the end of her first week as the learned Miss Wythe, found herself remembering details of the events of that first day. First, Lady Drysdale's brougham had met her at the coaching stop. From the chaffing that came the coachman's way, the Drysdales were well known in the village.

The coachman supervised the tying on of her trunk, boldly lettered "D. Wythe, Alford." His manner was not far from sullen, and after a small civil overture, which received only a grunt in response, Lottie boarded the carriage and tried to maintain her calm. She had not expected when she fled Pentstable, in her most fanciful imaginings, to be here in some stranger's carriage going to a strange house with the object of playing governess to an unknown child.

While she was busily nurturing her small shoots of rebellion, she had considered that she might one day be required to earn her living as a governess. Pomfret Priory might be her last refuge, but it was so far out of the way that, once installed in her own house, she might well look forward to a life as a recluse. It would be a real effort to travel, and alone at that, save for, possibly, the elderly cousin now in residence, to Scarborough, to Tunbridge Wells, to Bath. She had herself seen and—to her own shame—scorned elderly maiden ladies pottering about the baths and the lecture rooms, looking out at the world from hungry eyes. Now the possibility that she might—at the end, as her mother had said—become another such slightly dotty and very lonely antiquated lady was like a cold fist clutching at her heart.

The ride to the Drysdale manor had been uneventful. The road lay through rolling hills, green in the valleys but turning brown on the summits. There had obviously been little rain in recent weeks. The dust that rolled up on the road behind the carriage could have hidden the approach of an army. A faint breeze arose and carried the dust off behind them, so that Lottie arrived at the Drysdale door displaying only a light gritty coating to tell of her journey.

Then had come the introduction to Lady Drysdale, a totally ineffectual woman in Lottie's opinion. Now, after a week at Drysdale House, Lottie could assess that first interview in a more knowledgeable way.

The clear master of the house was Sir Albin. His sudden, unexpected, and unwished-for return—the conjectural cause of which was discussed in whispered speculation in the servants' hall—was in truth owing to his engaging in a brawl rather more serious than ordinary.

"Mark my words," said Mrs. Linn, "he's done somebody a mischief and I'll not be surprised to see the Runners at the door."

"Hush yourself," said Penn severely, feeling the weight of his authority bearing down, "the master'll hear you and it'll be grievous bodily harm to *you*."

"He wouldn't. He takes good care of his neck, don't he? No chance of getting hisself hanged, not for just a servant," objected Parsons, but Lottie thought that Parsons' expression turned thoughtful, and just a touch worried.

And Lottie now remembered the abrupt meeting with

Sir Albin himself. "Take care of her," Lady Drysdale
had instructed Penn, and for a while Lottie had tried to
decipher the inner meaning of that remark, to discern
Lady Drysdale's worry.

It seemed perfectly clear to Lottie that the household
was a far-from-serene one. The servants were worried
but uncommunicative, Lady Drysdale was apprehensive. Even Delia had impressed upon Lottie, when
the governess took up the chore of walking Puff every
afternoon, not to turn over the outing to her step-
brother.

"Albin does not really like Puff," Delia told her. "I
don't believe," she added slowly, as though the thought
had just occurred to her, "he likes anybody."

7

HOW MUCH had changed in that first week! Lottie, to her own surprise, discovered that she enjoyed her new employment, but in particular she began to grow fond of her five-year-old charge.

Delia was a fretful, spoiled child, as was only natural in one who never went outdoors, never even left her third-floor aerie, and whose only company was servants. Although she was coddled by her maid, Bessie, as though she were Bessie's own, the child had little to occupy her days. Anyone, thought Lottie stoutly, would become querulous and pouty in the same circumstances.

Lottie spent her first night at Drysdale House in a turmoil the like of which she had never yet known. Deciding to leave home for a short term had been almost child's play compared with her current task. Never trained as a governess, of course, Lottie could only try to remember Miss Wythe's very short term of instruction while her own plain wardrobe was being made. Fortunately, Lottie had taken all her ready money with her.

And of course, as Miss Wythe pointed out, she would have her income as governess to spend. That remark brought on a spirited discussion, for Lottie had no intention of profiting by her kindness to Miss Wythe. The argument ended at last, Miss Wythe believing she had prevailed, and Lottie silently determined to turn over all her earnings to her governess.

Since the small hours of the night seemed to have

erased all memory of the guidance Miss Wythe had given Lottie, she was forced to recall Miss Wythe's procedures when she first came to Pentstable. Not until near morning did Lottie fall asleep.

Her first morning with Delia had not augured well. The girl scarcely spoke at first, regarding Lottie from the corners of her eyes with the obvious hope that her new instructress would vanish, the sooner the better.

However apprehensive Lottie had been before she arrived at the Drysdale manor, the knowledge that she was not Charlotte Forester, a young woman of no experience, but—as far as the Drysdale family knew—an experienced teacher who had been governess to young ladies of impeccable breeding, sustained her in her first overtures in her new position.

It was hard to remember now just how she had begun with Delia. It may have been sheer instinct, thought Lottie later, but fortunately she hit upon the one way to the child's heart. The first morning, after a breakfast consumed silently and alone in the servants' dining room, Lottie entered the schoolroom with a cheerfulness she was far from feeling.

The little terrier, clearly discerning Lottie's uneasiness, leapt from Delia's lap and advanced on the intruder, drawing up to his full height, somewhere around Lottie's ankles, and barking as fiercely as though he had a pack of wolves at his beck and call.

Lottie laughed. "Good morning, Delia. You have such a fierce protector, I vow I am quite frightened to death!"

Delia watched her warily. "He doesn't like strangers."

"Nor do you, I expect," said Lottie in a bracing tone. "I quite sympathize with you. I should not like someone coming in on me that I didn't know, with the purpose of arranging my future."

A true statement, of course, since it was that very

sentiment that had brought her to this place, in a disguise she was not yet comfortable with. "Do you think your protector will let me sit down?"

Delia did not answer. Lottie glanced at her swiftly. It was clear to Lottie that in all likelihood many a previous governess had been routed by Delia and her canine ally. How could she ever gain the girl's confidence? How could she even begin to teach a child whose every gesture spoke defiance?

Suddenly it was as though Miss Wythe herself stood at Lottie's elbow. "Begin as you mean to go on," the apparition was urging. "Will you let a dog small enough to hold in your hand send you packing?"

No! Lottie thought for a guilty moment that she had spoken aloud, but Delia gave no sign of having heard her. Lottie bent down and fixed the dog with her gaze. "What is his name?"

Grudgingly Delia said, "Puff."

Lottie regarded the furry gray creature thoughtfully. "I see, like a puff of smoke. A good name." She spoke quietly, looking into the suspicious doggy face, willing the animal to admit that she was harmless.

Delia said, surprised, "No one else ever guessed why I named him that."

"No? Well, Puff, you have sharp teeth but you won't use them on me, I assure you. Here—" She extended her hand to him slowly, and suddenly he stopped barking. Curiosity brought him forward to sniff at the fingers offered him, and in a moment his plumy tail moved back and forth. Lottie was inordinately satisfied. Imagine being ecstatic because a dog accepted you!

Nonetheless, it truly was the acchievement she thought it was. Delia's expression altered, and Lottie discerned a reluctant respect in the glance sent her way.

Lottie sat in a chair opposite Delia's. "I'd like to get better acquainted, Delia. Or do you prefer to be called Cordelia? That's such a lovely name."

"I'm called Delia," said the child. "Are you going to make me do sums and everything?"

Lottie smiled reassuringly. "Perhaps not at the first. But you know when you have your own establishment, you will need to know sums, in order to supervise your servants."

"I'll never have my own house," said Delia, "but if you want me to do sums, I shall." Lottie was delighted with the girl's capitulation, until she added, "There's nothing else to do up here."

Lottie asked questions to find out how much Delia had already been taught—so had Miss Wythe done when she arrived at Pentstable—and was appalled to find out the child could barely read, had no grasp of sums, and although the globe in the corner of the room was freshly dusted, it was obvious that Delia had not the slightest notion of what it represented.

"What did your previous governess teach you?" Lottie asked at last.

"Mostly they were afraid of Puff," said Delia candidly, "and they didn't stay long."

It seemed clear that Delia's education to this point had run along the lines of devising ways of disposing of unwanted tutors.

"Well," said Lottie pacifically, "I assure you that you will be much happier once you learn to get on with your studies. You may not be able to travel a great deal—"

"My brother Albin says that I'll never get out of this room," said Delia.

"Nonsense!"

"I've never even been to the village."

"The village!" said Lottie. "That's only six miles away. How would you like to know about Arabia Felix, or India?"

"What are they?"

"Countries far away." Lottie crossed to the globe.

Twirling it expertly—perhaps setting an example for the girl to emulate?—she pointed. "Here is where we are. And here is India. And Arabia is just here."

"I don't see anything special. How can I know anything about that, except that it is orange?"

"Arabia is not orange at all!" cried Lottie. "It is tan, and brown, and gray, and sometimes very bright green!"

Delia looked suspiciously at the orange area on the globe. "How do you know that? Have you been there?"

"No, not I. But people who have been to these places write books about their travels. And once you learn to read well, the entire world opens up for you. Not just India, this red place, or Arabia. Let's see what books you have."

The bookshelf, only one, and that inconveniently located under the window, held a mere handful of books. Lottie discovered that they showed little wear, mute evidence of the short tenure of previous instructresses. She saw a couple of her own favorites, and some, like Mangnall's *Historical and Miscellaneous Questions for the Use of Young People*, which she remembered with a shudder of distaste. A boring book, she recalled, with odd bits of information jumbled together without order, most of which she could not now summon to mind.

Well, she would just have to do her best for Miss Wythe's sake, and for the first two weeks of her employment she made great progress, or, more precisely, her charge did.

"I think," said Lottie after the first few days of instructions, "that there is plenty of time later to learn"—reading from the preface of Mangnall's textbook—"the chronological order of the kings of England, and they have certainly forgotten three queens, haven't they? And all the Roman emperors—I suspect you are not at all interested in them, isn't that right?''

They were sitting in Delia's third-floor sitting room. The windows were closed, in consideration of Delia's fragile health, but Lottie set the door ajar. Lest we both smother, she had remarked. Now Delia nodded, her golden curls bouncing in her confirmation of her boredom with the lessons so far presented to her.

This Miss Wythe was quite the nicest governess she had ever had, one who seemed to know how to make reading interesting, and best of all, one who understood about Puff. In truth, were Delia not the nice child she was, she might have been jealous of her governess, for Puff, feeling that Miss Wythe was present on his account as much as that of his mistress, came to believe that his chosen position was at the feet of this young lady who knew just how to scratch that particular place on the top of his head, and just when to say, "Good dog." Puff was convinced that he had entered into his own conception of heaven.

"I think I shall ask your mama to send to London for a few volumes that I know you will like. They are quite new, but my own dear governess, Miss W—" She stopped short, her breath stopped in her throat. How nearly she had given herself away! Or rather, had almost given Miss Wythe away. She was becoming too comfortable in her new situation. She had become overly confident, and that would never do. Quickly she spoke again, intending a diversion from her nearly fatal slip of the tongue. "Miss Edgeworth has written some entertaining tales for young students—"

Puff took exception to his surroundings suddenly, and sprang to his feet, facing the door and barking energetically.

At the same moment, the door was pushed inward, and Sir Albin Drysdale stood on the threshold.

"Entertaining? You are not here to entertain my

sister," he said. He was not above average height, nor
was he of particularly stocky build, but somehow he
seemed much too large for the room. Lottie,
remembering her place, stood and tried to appear
respectful.

"No, Sir Albin—" she began, but Puff had not
ceased barking, and she found it difficult, not to say
undignified, to make herself heard.

Since the dog had placed himself protectively in
front of his young mistress, it was easy for Delia to
reach down and pick him up. In a moment he was
quieted.

"You were saying?" Albin's voice held contempt. As
though, he seemed to say, anything a mere governess,
lower-class and female (so went his thoughts), could be
of interest to him.

"As I am sure you are aware, Sir Albin, a child learns
much more quickly when she is interested in the subject
at hand."

"Ah, but that is not the whole of it," rasped Sir
Albin. "What should she be learning? That is the true
question at bottom. She will never have her own household, she will not go into society. And why should she
even be taught at all?"

Lottie did not know, afterward, how she held her
temper, how she was able to refrain from hurling
Mangnall's *Questions*, which she found still in her
hand, at his head. But fortunately in time she realized
that this was precisely the reaction he was trying to
provoke in her—to instill in her a feeling of fear lest she
be dismissed out of hand, a feeling of inferiority, in
fact, a condition that could lead to mistakes, and a real
cause of dismissal. And Miss Wythe's reputation as a
first-rate governess might be sadly tarnished.

If Lottie were ever to feel inferior to anyone, it would
not be this jumped-up, dandyish person! She, more by
chance than design, found the right answer.

"Because Lady Drysdale has engaged me to instruct her."

A glint in Sir Albin's pale blue eyes told her she had scored. He stood there a further moment looking at her, and then sent his words darting toward his half-sister. "Keep that mutt away from me, Delia, or you won't have him long."

He was gone in a moment. Puff, remaining victorious on the field, essayed a few triumphant barks, but Delia, her hands shaking, tightened her grip on his muzzle.

"He'll do what he says, too, Miss Wythe. And you must know that Puff detests him—"

"With reason, I expect."

"And even Mama cannot defy him. He has the money, you see, and we have none."

Alertly seeking a diversion, besides being a true daughter of her time, Lottie queried, "Did she not have a dowry? Surely she has some funds?"

"I think Albin has it all now," said Delia in a small voice. "I do not know precisely how it happened, but poor Mama said once she does not have funds to get us away."

Suddenly realizing that she had shown an unwarranted curiosity, Lottie sat down abruptly. Her knees were trembling, and for some reason she felt soiled. Even while reassuring her charge, her thoughts moved on business of their own, and she at last recognized the source of her uneasiness.

Unaccustomed to society she might be, and naive she certainly was, but she recognized, at last, the quality of Sir Albin's stare. He saw her not as his sister's governess, a sort of upper servant, or as a preceptress with whom he might discuss the philosophy of education. No! He saw her as an undressed female, denuded of clothing by his impertinent and degrading glance.

This—she felt sure—was a situation that dear Miss Wythe would not have fallen into, at least recently. Lottie realized further that she was without friends save for servants with much more to lose than she had. She was on her own in this household.

This was not, strictly speaking, true. In another week she had prevailed on Lady Drysdale to send to London for a box of books she was familiar with from her own quite recent schooldays. Miss Edgeworth's *Moral Tales* would be accompanied by *Popular Tales*, that author's contribution to the entertainment of children from seven to seventeen, according to the title pages.

Joining those books would be Mrs. Mary Martha Sherwood's *The Fairchild Family* and *Little Henry and His Bearer*, promising hours of pleasant reading while Delia learned enough to try more difficult volumes.

If, of course, Lottie were able to hold her position for that length of time! Besides the risk of her disguise being penetrated, there was also the very real danger of Lady Forester's sending a peremptory summons for her. While Lottie maintained that she was an independent heiress, with a home of her own to repair to as a last resort, she dreaded the ignominy of her mother's ordering her as though she were no older than Delia herself.

Miss Wythe had taken upon herself the task of informing Lady Forester that Lottie was well, and if her missive led Lottie's mother to assume that the girl was safe with Miss Wythe in Alford, it was not Miss Wythe's fault, at least not entirely.

Not daily, but more frequently than not, Sir Albin appeared in Delia's suite on the top floor. He seemed to know that his presence was unwelcome, but his only response was a grin. But he made no trouble, and Lottie learned to return his impertinent gaze with a level stare of her own. She was more alert now than she had been before, when she was still unsuspecting and unwary, and she could often recognize Puff's awareness of the hated man's approach.

Upon a signal from Lottie, Delia would scoop up the dog and keep him quiet, thus giving Sir Albin one less irritation. He told them he had come to supervise his sister's education, but while that was patently not true, Lottie could not believe there was any other reason for his visits. If she had had any pretense to beauty, she might have become suspicious, but an ordinary girl such as she was? Nonsense! She had been told too many times that she was plain, unattractive, lacking in feminine curves and the allure that such curves provided, and thus considered herself beyond male notice, to say nothing of masculine interest.

Perhaps a week had passed from the first visit to the schoolroom. Her days with Delia had settled into a pattern. Delia was helped out of her bed in the mornings by her dear maid Bessie, dressed, and placed in the chair in her sitting room in which she would spend the day. Puff was taken for his walk by an underfootman, and then returned to spend the day with the two creatures he loved the most.

Lottie's breakfast was brought to her, and she and Delia ate their luncheon together. In midafternoon, Bessie put Delia to bed for her nap, and Lottie was free for a couple of hours.

Used to country ways, she clung to her free time as though to a life raft rescuing her from the stuffy tedium of Delia's schoolroom. She walked in the woods, in rain or sun, her excuse being to take Puff for his walk. "Sure Sam'll be glad to do it," protested Mrs. Linn the first two or three days that Lottie stopped in the kitchen to tell the servants where she would be.

"I'm glad to do it too." Lottie smiled, and won a friend in both Mrs. Linn and in Sam, the second footman.

After a week of walking in the home park in the late afternoon, letting Puff trot importantly around the shrubbery and sniff suspiciously at tracks Lottie could not see, she watched in surprise as Puff stopped short, lifted his head, and sniffed the air. Suddenly he whined, and abandoned the interesting scent he had been following on the ground. He came to Lottie and pressed against her skirt, all the time gazing at a spot in the woods.

"What is it, boy? What do you see?"

His only answer was a whine. Lottie scrutinized the trees with a suspicion equal to Puff's, but could see nothing, not even a hint of movement of man or beast. But Lottie was not foolish, and she was willing to take Puff's word for it—something in the woods he did not like.

"Let's go back," she said to Puff. This was an expression he knew, and in the past he had joyfully described capering arabesques in front of her as they made their laggard way to the house. This time he followed at her heels, and more than once he looked over his shoulder in the way they had come.

That there was something unpleasant in the woods, she had no doubt. A fox, she guessed, or even a poacher daring to set his snares in daylight.

She mentioned the possibility to Mrs. Linn when they returned to the house. "Probably nothing to worry about, but I thought I should tell someone."

"Sir Albin is away for the day," said Mrs. Linn. "No, there's nothing to worry about."

Lottie was not sure she followed the cook's reasoning, but it was, after all, none of her business. Later she would wonder how she could have been so mistaken.

8

I N THE third week after Lottie's arrival at the Drysdale estate, she began to realize that her thoughts were not entirely taken up by the child with whom she spent most of her time. Her walks in the woodland, in the home park, and even along the carefully trimmed edges of the herb garden were kept short.

She knew that Sir Albin had not been at home that day when Puff had taken such an active dislike to whatever it was he sensed in the woods. She doubted that Sir Albin had doubled back to lie in wait for her in his own woods. Besides, Puff's reaction had been defiant when he met Sir Albin in Delia's rooms. Of course, he was defending his mistress, and perhaps out in the open, so to speak, he had a realistic sense of peril. How ridiculous such a thought was!

But there had indeed been something untoward in the woods that day, and whoever—or whatever—it was, she was sure she did not wish to become further acquainted.

At least Sir Albin had given up his frequent visits to the schoolroom. She could be grateful for that change of mind in him. But still she could not shake the strange feeling of unease that the very house instilled in her. It was as though the sour cast of Sir Albin's mind, at least as it was revealed to Lottie, had infiltrated even the walls of the huge house.

For the first time she began to think seriously about returning to Pentstable.

Delia was, she suspected, in all likelihood the nicest of

all the children that Lottie might encounter in thirty years of life as a governess. Miss Wythe's thirty years had not always been spent in halcyon situation. Even at Pentstable, Carrie had proved incorrigible, even though Lottie's mother had been the kindest of employers.

Perhaps, Lottie mused, one afternoon as she set out for a walk across the broad lawn with the intention of reaching a coppice she had never examined before, perhaps I should have considered Pomfret more particularly. After all, if I went to live at Pomfret, there was no real reason why I could not leave Pomfret when I chose.

Certaily she would be her own mistress at Pomfret. Gresham Manor nearby—which could have been her home, had she not fled—was as far away from society as Pomfret, and yet no one considered that in marrying Mr. North she would be retiring from the world!

The only good thing that had come out of her flight to Alford, besides her immediate avoidance of the stranger who clearly had designs on her—her property, rather!— was that she could be of assistance to dear Miss Wythe.

The doctor had said that a month of treatment would bring the ailing limb very near to a total cure. Lottie had been three weeks here, and in another sennight she might consider seriously how to extricate herself from this unwanted position. She must take care, however, not to become so attached to her charge that she could not bear to leave her.

Her thoughts, allowed to drift in a most irresponsible way, took her back to Pentstable. What had her mother done when she learned that Lottie had vanished? Had she been furious with her? The answer to that question was obvious. Of course she had been! The only question was: how long would that anger last?

Lottie had written to her as soon as she had arrived at Alford. Miss Wythe had surely written to Lady Forester since then. Her mother knew she was safe, and by the time Lottie returned, the sharp edge of her mother's disappointment would have dulled.

She was sure that by this time Lady Monteagle's protégé would have given up his unwanted pursuit of her, and she could safely take up her life at home again. Carrie screaming and throwing objects when she didn't get her own way . . . Lady Forester, doting on her beautiful daughter, unable to stand against Carrie's demands . . . Lottie trying vainly to keep the peace, serving mostly as useful drudge . . .

Perhaps marriage would have been better? A quick vision sprang to her mind: Mr. North below her, head turned away, that small curl at the nape of his neck as he leaned forward. No! The force of her denial somewhat startled her. But she was right: a union of properties had no charm for her.

In her abstraction, she had traveled farther than she intended. The coppice, as she neared, was seen to be at the bottom of a small drop in the land. Puff had gone off on his own affairs, and she recalled hearing him back sometime before, and stop, as though his quarry had escaped him. She could see the tops of the trees, which she had believed to be mere saplings. The large trunks were hidden by the fold in the ground.

She looked back at the house. It was nearly out of sight, veiled by a hedge and other plantings. She had not looked at the building from this point of view before, and for a startled moment she did not recognize it.

Her free time was nearly gone. She would save the coppice for another day. She retraced her way a few steps. Puff did not come bounding to her as usual.

She whistled, then called. He did not appear.

"That foolish dog!" she said under her breath. Supposing him to have gone ahead to explore the grove of trees, she turned and strolled slowly toward it, calling.

Hearing no answer, she went to the edge of the hill.

Below her everything was still. Abnormally still, she thought, not a leaf stirring, not the breath of a breeze. Nor did she hear any excited canine whimperings, as if Puff were on the trail of a scurrying creature.

Lottie was no stranger to rough ground. She had walked over, climbed over, run over every inch of Pentstable land. If Puff were indeed somewhere in the trees below her, he was hurt, caught in a trap, killed by a badger—else he would have come to her.

Holding up her skirt in one hand, she braced herself with the other and slid down the steep incline to the ground below. She was at once in a shadowy place. Tree trunks stretched upward as though she stood in the center of a cathedral, and overhead the treetops formed a thick canopy, screening out the light.

"Puff?" she called, her voice oddly hushed.

Suddenly she heard the barest of unidentifiable sounds, followed instantly by a muffled voice—she was sure it was a human voice!

"Who's there?"

She advanced several steps into the trees. Suddenly the grove erupted around her.

She heard a footstep behind her, and started to turn, but not in time. An arm was flung from behind her, around her throat, and she fell backward. Her head hit the ground with force, and for a moment tears blinded her. She was aware of a flurry of strenuous activity just next to her.

She blinked the tears away, and saw Albin's face not six inches from her own. She screamed.

"You bitch!" snarled Sir Albin. "I'll show you—"

What he wished to show her was not to be known. She mustered her strength and tried to roll from beneath him, but he held her in a painful grip. He loosed one hand to tear at her bodice. That was a mistake.

Suddenly he howled in agony and fell away from her. She wasted no time in trying to understand what was

happening. She scurried to one side and scrambled to
her feet. She ran to the gravelly hillside down which she
had come only moments before, and got halfway up
before the sounds behind her took on a new quality and
she turned to look.

Sir Albin was on his feet, holding one hand with the
other and moving around in agitated steps. Dashing
around him, taking care not to encounter his flailing
feet was—Puff!

Now she understood. Sir Albin lying in wait, Puff
discovering him and barking a warning before the man
muzzled him. But Sir Albin needed two hands to subdue
Lottie, and Puff was free to bite the hand that held him.

Dreadfully afraid for the dog, Lottie screamed.
"Puff! Come away!"

She turned and clambered up to the top of the rise.
Below her she could see Puff still on the attack. Sir
Albin's foot at last connected with the furry gray ribs,
and the dog yelped in pain.

"Puff! Come!" She put all her authority into the two
words, and was rewarded. Puff came limping up the
slope, and she picked him up.

If he had been human, Lottie thought, that odd look
on the muzzle of the gray dog would have been a smile
of complete self-satisfaction!

9

SIR ALBIN Drysdale was sorely wounded.

He suffered not only in the calf of his leg, above his half-boots, the target of Puff's desire for revenge for a myriad of past insults, but also in his self-esteem.

He was an insensitive man. It had never before occurred to him that a woman might refuse his masterful advances. Most women, he admitted honestly, would have given in and then expected a certain largess from their traducers. And, to be completely accurate, the women he had had dealing with were, for the most part, not only far from inexperienced but also, in their expectation of recompense, not disappointed.

Sir Albin's money had come easily to him, and he did not begrudge its expenditure in his own pursuits.

Never did he make advances to a young lady of status. First, he was not yet ready to fall into parson's mousetrap, and certainly a lady of quality would not dally with him until after the vows had been spoken.

But governesses were a species apart. A governess was a member of a certain level of society, not precisely quality, but neither was she a servant. Insisting on making her living in a genteel fashion, a governess was still not eligible for marriage into the higher reaches of society.

Lottie was not the first governess to come in his way, but he had little enough notion of her true quality. He saw only a drably dressed woman, no figure to speak of, with no pretensions to superior birth and breeding. And since at the moment he dared not return to London lest the friends of the man he had beaten nearly to death take exception to his presence, he must make do with the talent at hand.

To his dismay, not only had Delia's stupid canine bitten him but also the governess herself had spurned him. He had the strongest conviction that just as she had fended off his advances in the woods, she would in all likelihood be excessively cautious not to be caught unaware in such a fashion again.

Well, Albin told himself, there was more than one way to bring the wench to heel. That expression of contempt for him that he had seen in her splendid eyes would be changed into fear and submissiveness, or he was sadly mistaken. He gloated over the prospect.

The next morning he limped into his stepmother's morning sitting-room, his purpose firmly in mind. Almost without taking note of it, he saw in Lady Drysdale's eyes the alarm and helplessness that he was accustomed to seeing. There was no question, he thought with satisfaction, as to who was master in this house!

"G-good morning, Albin," Lady Drysdale said nervously. She was not accustomed to his company so early in the morning, and, as she had learned that any deviation from his self-indulgent ways would inevitably lead to unpleasantness, or worse, for her, she steeled herself against his demands.

"You've made a mistake," said Albin with a slight sneer, "as usual. It is *not* a good morning."

Oh dear, she thought, and searched her conscience swiftly. What could be amiss now?

"But you will make it better at once. That foolish governess must go."

"Oh dear!" she said, this time aloud. "The first one we have had that Delia likes!"

"That should tell you how lax she is. That young miss has no desire to learn, I can tell you. I have made it my business to oversee some of her lessons. Ma'am, I am appalled."

Albin was enjoying himself. Lady Drysdale could only utter small mewing objections, and he drove on.

"Indeed, I see no reason for the child to have a governess at all. You know she'll be a useless invalid all her life, however short it may be. Besides, she's only a female. What is the use of teaching her anything?"

Lady Drysdale's fears spoke to her. She had never liked her stepson, from the first day she came here, newly wed, to live. He had been an obnoxious little boy, malicious and sly, and the happiest day of her married life was the day he was sent away to Oxford.

There had been an incident—Delia's nurse had told her she had found him bending over the baby's cradle, his hands active within. She had not seen precisely what he was doing, but Lady Drysdale had her own convictions.

In order to convince Albin's father to send him away to school, she had been required to dismiss the nurse without references. But the subsequent peace of mind, she believed, was worth the sacrifice.

Lady Drysdale had not forgotten the incident. Every time Albin mentioned her daughter, she searched for ominous overtones, and whether she was accurate or not, she usually found them. So it was now.

"But I am paying the governess's wages from my own money."

"And a waste of good coin it is, too."

"She is so good with Delia, and I dread telling the child she must part with her."

Albin, knowing precisely his stepmother's weaknesses, said in a casual tone, "She will have that foolish dog to comfort her. Unless, of course, the dog runs into an accident of some kind."

Hearing it put that way, Lady Drysdale saw her duty clearly. She knew that governesses, although they never stayed after they arrived at the manor, were nonetheless easy enough to find. But Delia's affections were entirely engaged by that diminutive animal.

"Very well," she sighed. "I shall give her her notice."

"At once, if you please," he said, amiable enough now that he had gained his objective. "I shall be away for a few days, and she must be gone before I leave."

Lottie received the news of her dismissal calmly. In truth, she had been expecting it since her encounter with Sir Albin in the woods. She assessed him correctly as a man with a short temper and an exaggerated sense of what was due his dignity, and certainly she had not catered to the latter. Perhaps, she thought, if Puff had not come to her rescue and sunk his teeth into the tempting leg, he might have overlooked her defiance.

But then, she realized soberly, had the dog not come to her rescue, she could not have resisted the man's great strength.

Stooping to give Puff a caress on the top of his shaggy little head, she gave herself over to comforting her young charge.

"But why?" demanded Delia between sobs. "You have done nothing! I won't have it, I won't!"

At length Delia's storms subsided to hiccups, and Lottie, continuing to stroke the girl's hair, could turn to her own thoughts. What would she do next? She must go back to Miss Wythe in Alford and confess failure. Not only in holding down a simple employment for a mere month but also in damaging Miss Wythe's excellent reputation. Lady Drysdale had clearly indicated that the fault was not Lottie's, but she gave no indication that she would say as much in whatever references she gave her.

But beyond her return, defeated, to Miss Wythe, Lottie must after that return to Pentstable and brave whatever storms her absence had raised. She did not look forward to doing so.

She did not quite recognize the fact, but she had for a few weeks been in charge of her own life. This did not mean that she was not subject to oversight. All the time she knew full well she was an employee, and therefore subject to dismissal, and now it had come. But before that, she had been free of her mother's constant complaints against her. She had not heard for more than a fortnight how ugly she was. Sir Albin, clearly, had thought she was sufficiently attractive to stalk her in the woods.

Even so, she knew it was because she was young and female and dependent. But if she had been *truly* ugly, would he have noticed her? It was something of a puzzle, but somewhere within her something stirred. She could not recognize it yet, but she thought it might turn out to be a realization that her mother was mistaken.

At any rate, she was of two minds about returning to Pentstable. Mr. North still existed somewhere in England, and she did not know where. Had he remained around Pentstable, waiting for her return? If so, it would be a tactical mistake to return before he was well and truly out of the running for her hand in marriage, as Lady Monteagle had assured Lady Forester he was.

Besides, her mother knew she had gone to Miss Wythe's, and was perfectly capable of descending upon Alford and dragging her erring daughter home without ceremony.

One thing was certain: she must leave the Drysdale house at once. It was the next day before she had packed her trunk and seen it roped onto the back of an open curricle. The tag was clearly legible: D. Wythe, and the address. She said good-bye to Delia, to Lady Drysdale, who did not meet her eyes, and to the servants.

"In good time for the coach, miss," said Goff, the groom, as he helped her to mount to the seat. In a few moments they were on their way to the village coaching station. And from there, where? She did not know.

She had only a few coins in her small reticule, feeling it advisable to store her wages, given to her yesterday, in the trunk. She would not be tempted to spend the money on the way to Alford, and she could give it intact to Miss Wythe.

The day was sunny and warm. This was pleasant country she rode through, she thought. She had essayed a few words to the groom, but his answer came in the form of a grunt or two, so she gave up.

How peaceful these three weeks had been, she thought with regret. Except, of course, for the harassment of Sir Albin, they had been ideal. She had been valued by Delia, adored by small Puff, and—she was realizing it a little late—had not heard every day a catalog of her recent shortcomings.

Well, it did no good to repine over misfortune. She had had a taste of freedom and had liked it. But her brief fling was over, and she must return to Alford. The money she had in her reticule was sufficient for the fare and for refreshments on the way if the coach were delayed.

The sun was warm on her back, the rhythm of the hooves was soothing, and her companion required no attention. Lottie drifted into a kind of dreamlike state. They met no one on the road, which curved around small rises and past little clumps of trees.

The road now descended into a modest valley, at the bottom of which lay a coppice of trees. At the lowest part of the road was a narrow bridge over a stream. They slowed almost to a stop to cross the narrow bridge. She looked down into the water. The bed was nearly dry at this time of year, although the banks showed that it might run high in spring-flood time.

Just then she caught sight, from the corner of her eye, a movement among the trees, very close to the road. She looked quickly, and grabbed the groom's sleeve in sudden alarm.

"Now, then, miss, what be ye doing? Scare the horse, that's what!"

"Look, Goff!" she said sharply, and pointed.

Someone stood just off the road, in the shadow cast by some underbrush. A highwayman?

Impossible. Even as she told herself no highwayman would think it worthwhile to ambush a curricle containing two servants and a trunk, far from the main road, the figure stepped into the road ahead of them and gestured with what was quite the largest pistol she had ever seen.

She screamed. The groom uttered an oath and pulled back on the reins.

The masked man grabbed at the bridle of the horse, fixed his eyes—as far as she could tell through the holes in his mask—on her, and growled, "Get down!"

She was never sure just in what order things happened next. She knew she shouted at the servant, "Do something!" But even as she did so, she knew he was too petrified to move. Something had to be done. She reached abruptly across the groom for the whip in the socket. She saw as in a dream the groom falling off the seat, impelled accidentally by her lunge for the whip, and she knew, although she did not have time to watch, that he fell slowly but inexorably to the ground. The reins were loose now, and trailed across the floor.

In one gesture she picked up the reins, just in time. The horse, alarmed by the activities around him, which he did not understand, and feeling free of the groom's firm hand on the reins, reared and whinnied. The masked man loosed his hold on the bridle and leapt to the side, away from the flailing and deadly hooves.

And Lottie grasped at her chance, reins in left hand, whip in right. She raised the whip over her head and brought it down with purpose upon the mask. The man, seeing the whip descending, raised his arm to ward off the blow.

Lottie blessed the old coachman who had taught her all he knew about driving. Bringing the reins taut gradually, and spurring the beast on with judiciously light touches of the whip, she urged the horse, nothing loath, to headlong flight. Glancing back over her shoulder as they rounded the bend at the top of the hill, she saw the groom prone on the grassy verge at the end of the bridge and the highwayman sitting in the middle of the lane, rocking back and forth, his hands covering his face in agony.

10

LOTTIE HAD no need to whip up the horse. Already frightened out of his wits, he had no purpose but to flee whatever danger he saw in his mind. Indeed, as excellent a whip as Lottie was, she had all she could do to ride out the careening journey of the curricle.

She pulled on the reins until she thought her arm would leap from its socket. She still held the whip in her right hand, even though by now she was scarcely aware of it. They were up the hill from the small bridge where the highwayman had appeared from the woods, and around the bend before she could draw breath.

The horse was terrified. Only a strong hand on the reins could bring him to a halt, could tell him that someone else was in control and no harm would befall him.

Behind Lottie sprawled the victims of the ambush. Burned on her mind was the vision of the robber himself, rocking in pain. Pain, she knew, from the savage lash of her whip. How could she, a person who spurned violence as though it were brought by the devil, or at least by those who knew no better, raise that whip and bring it down on a human more ferociously than ever she would strike a horse?

Suddenly it was as though she stood outside herself, the old submissive Lottie watching while the driver of this curricle, disciple obviously of Jehu, careened down the narrow road like a mad thing. The old Lottie experienced one unsettling, really *jarring* moment when she did not recognize her other—perhaps a new?—self. The moment passed, however, in the necessities of flight.

While she was rapidly leaving the coachman and the robber in her wake, she had no illusions that she was soon to reach safety. First of all she did not know precisely the directions to the coaching inn where she was to take passage back to Alford. The horse was now slowing, breathing in great gusts, but the danger of a runaway disaster was clearly past.

She could look around her and take stock of her situation. She had been forced to stand the whole time after the coachman had departed, in order to exercise her full strength on controlling the horse. She brought the horse now to a halt, his sides heaving, and blowing heavily. At last she was able to sit down, both she and her steed having reached a state of exhaustion.

What was she to do?

Goff, the groom, was far behind, and at last view he lay supine on the verge of the road. He had been no help during the robbery, and no one could suspect his behavior would improve now. Although she thought she had seen him begin to stir, she was sure it would take some time for him to recover.

She had no doubt that he would be on his way, as soon as he could stand, either back to the Drysdale house to report the event, or ahead to the inn, probably following the tracks of the horse and curricle, to regain possession of the Drysdale property. She was certain that her safety was not paramount in the groom's thinking.

One thing was certain. There would be no welcome for her at the Drysdales'. Accident or not, holdup notwithstanding, she believed she would be turned away at Sir Albin's direction. Nor would her pride permit risking such a rejection.

There was something else that nagged at her mind that she could not quite catch hold of. Something seen —or rather, as it turned out, something *not* seen. She looked over her shoulder. The boot was empty. The trunk was gone!

Gone! All her wordly possessions—that is, all the possessions of Miss D. Wythe of Alford—had been tumbled off in that wild ride. She knew she should have seen to the ropes herself. That Goff! Some incompetence would not be suffered at Pentstable!

And all her own money too—or rather Miss D. Wythe's—which she had secreted in the trunk for safekeeping!

She must go back and get the trunk. She could not take passage on a stagecoach without any baggage! She glanced down at her skirt. Where she had leaned against the dashboard—a large brown streak of dirt all across the front. One sleeve torn on the whip socket, and her face . . . While she could not see her face, she remembered wiping a dirty hand across her mouth in the excitement of the runaway, and she did not doubt she looked like the veriest ragamuffin! She needed her trunk.

She even began to turn the curricle, when a wiser thought stopped her. For one, she was not sure she could even lift the trunk onto the boot—certainly not and keep the fractious steed under control. She had a quick vision of the trunk, safely tied again on the vehicle, being carried down the road out of sight while she stood in the road where her trunk had been. Of the two—trunk and herself—she preferred to leave the trunk behind.

She would quite simply have to go ahead to the coaching inn and make whatever excuses she could think of for her gutter-child appearance. She could pay for her passage with the coins she had in her pocket, and trust the Drysdales to forward the trunk to the address plainly displayed on it. Miss Wythe would suffer no loss, and Lottie would recover the money she had earned on behalf of her dear friend.

Gently she set the horse again in motion. Feeling a sure hand again on the reins, he gave no trouble, and was no doubt too exhausted to make another grand run. Now, as her own thoughts became less riotous, reason asserted itself. Ahead of her lay the coaching inn, near neighbor of the Drysdale lands. And she, a stranger, would drive up in a Drysdale curricle, without groom, abigail, or baggage, and take the stage to Alford.

It was difficult to see how she could explain her state to anyone who might inquire. She would certainly find it difficult to sustain the suspicious stares of other passengers, and possibly the coachman himself might decline to take her, fearing pursuit for harboring a malefactor of some description.

Suddenly the word "pursuit" burst upon her with clarity. She was in truth being pursued, even now. Her hand jerked on the reins, and the animal in front of her protested. The little niggling idea that had lurked at the corners of her mind came into the open. Pursuit indeed!

What she now remembered was the one thing that made her situation entirely different. Awkward to say the least, possibly even dangerous. She set herself to relive the entire episode, from the moment she first caught sight of movement in the woods. The highwayman had stepped out into the road, his face masked, one hand holding that enormous gun. Something had caught her eye.

The hand. That was it, the *other* hand! The right hand holding the pistol—bare of glove, it was a well-cared for, *clean* hand, not that of a villain as she conceived him. But the hand that gestured—that other hand!

The left hand that gestured to her impatiently to

alight from the vehicle wore a ring on the little finger. A ring, moreover, that she had had more than one occasion to note. A dark red stone, carved curiously, set in gold. Not that she could see the carving from where she had sat, frozen in fear, but the red glint she remembered, and, given the circumstances, she was as sure as she was of her own name that the highwayman was none other than Sir Albin Drysdale!

She drew a deep, calming breath that failed of its purpose. She was not calm. In all likelihood she would not become calm for some time. As proof, her inner vision showed her a scene that could properly be called a disaster. She arriving at the inn, Sir Albin following, spouting lies about her. She had had plenty of experience in only a short time in regard to his cavalier regard for truth.

And she could expect no help from the innkeeper or his boys. Sir Albin would be the law in these parts. And since she now believed, with the force of sudden conviction, that he was bent on her destruction, it would certainly not be sensible to put herself again in his hands.

For perhaps a mile she labored under a strong sense of injustice. She had done nothing to him, save refuse to accept his advances. Had she wanted to indulge in unconventional behavior with a stranger, she could have accepted Marcus North!

Suddenly she had a vision of the man below her in the entrance hall at Pentstable. Broad shoulders, neatly dressed hair, an impression of latent strength. To her own surprise, she giggled. She would wager that Marcus North would make short work of Sir Albin!

Horrified at the way her mind was working, she pulled it back to the point, with some difficulty. She was driving what could easily be regarded as a stolen rig, she had left the groom behind without stopping to see whether he was alive or dead, and without her trunk to

bolster her story of leaving Drysdale House on
legitimate business, she might well find herself in
prison.

Or worse.

She had no clear idea of how the penal system
worked, nor did she have the slightest inclination to find
out. She must get right away from Drysdale country.

Nor, now that she knew who the highwayman was,
did she feel she would be safe with Miss Wythe. Her
trunk gave the address where Sir Albin could lay hands
on her. Besides, she could not put Miss Wythe into
danger. Sir Albin might well descend upon Alford, but
if she herself were not there, he might depart without
harming the elderly governess.

Dismayed, Lottie began to feel she was being
bombarded by unwelcome thoughts, like a fortress
under siege. And she was uneasily aware that her
defenses were in danger of crumbling.

The first consideration, one that required intensive
thought, was how to leave Drysdale country. Only
secondarily did she think about in which direction to
start. At the moment, the only desirable direction was
away.

If the stage to Alford were forbidden to her, then she
must go in another direction. But first, she must divest
herself of the telltale horse and vehicle, clearly recognizable as Drysdale property. She pulled the horse to a
stop and dropped lightly to the ground. She led the
animal a few yards off the roadway, not hidden, but
equally not in plain view, and looped the reins lightly
around a branch. If the rig were not found soon, the
branch could easily be broken by a horse determined to
return to his stable.

She walked along the road to the next rise and
surveyed the possibilities. She was still, she judged,
perhaps four miles from the coaching inn. It was a good
thing that she was a countrywoman and walking long

distances was an everyday occurrence for her. She left the roadway and started along the edge of a plowed field in the general direction of the inn. Walking along the road would surely be easier, but also she would be more vulnerable to any pursuit.

No, it would be a long way around, but in some way she must avoid the inn. She dared not for her life take a chance on being discovered by Albin Drysdale. The rhythm of her steps did what nothing else had accomplished. She began to think calmly, and with some purpose. The inn lay on the road back to Alford, of course. But also, toward the north, the road would lead in all likelihood to Pomfret—or more accurately to a town nearby.

Pomfret up to this point in her life had seemed like the end of the earth, a place so far out of the mainstream of life that deliberately removing oneself to that place was equivalent to taking up residence in a hermit's shack in the forest. So much had her ideas changed that, at this moment, Pomfret Priory took on the attributes of sanctuary at a medieval altar. And Pomfret would not release her to her enemy after forty days!

While Lottie had been fending off the unwelcome advances of the master of the house, Marcus North, in his rooms in London, now unaccountably dismal, was engaged in the attempt to repel some of the most depressing thoughts of his life. It was strange, he thought, that a young lady he had never laid eyes on would fill his thoughts almost to the exclusion of all else.

In his recent conversations here in London, upon his return from Pentstable, with Annabella Fitzhugh, and with several other young ladies whose names were gone beyond recall and whose faces remained dim and blurry in his memory, he had learned one thing that he had not known before. He knew now that he would not be able to sustain an interest in such trivial conversation as the ladies provided him for even three months' betrothal time.

Since Miss Charlotte Forester had made no secret of the fact that she did not even wish to meet him, he had looked upon the world with altered vision. Since Lottie —he called her that in his mind, since he had heard the family speak of her so—had dismissed him unseen, he was unpleasantly surprised to find that certain young ladies, not in their first Seasons, had been more than eager to speak to him, to flirt with him.

And, being essentially a prosy and commonsensical man, he looked outside himself to discover where the attraction lay. And inevitably he came to the conclusion that it had to be in his fortune. He was not a nabob having wealth beyond the dreams of Avarice, as the good Dr. Johnson had put it, but he was more than comfortably fixed, and his wife and family—supposing he ever attained such felicity—would want for nothing.

But, bearing his cousin Geoffrey's experience in mind, he was not ready to marry for the sake of marrying and producing heirs. He realized that it was time to come to terms with Lottie's rejection. Surely it was not anything that could come clear to him in London.

He gave orders to pack up his effects, summoned his groom, and, driving himself in his curricle, set out on the Great North Road for Gresham, where a man could think, and no silly women flirted with him.

He did not intend to travel swiftly, nor did he. Thus it was that he arrived at a small inn where a stagecoach was preparing to depart for Alford. There seemed to be some bustle in the yard, beyond what was the normal complement to a stagecoach's arrival and departure.

Giving the reins to his groom, he squinted at the sun lowering in the west and said, "I think we'll stay the night here. It looks not too down at heel, and I'm not fond of traveling without a full moon."

He entered the public room of the inn, to find a sorry sight. A man, obviously a servant, was leaning against the bar nursing a drink that was already half-gone. Marcus thought it was not his first of the afternoon. A darkening bruise on his left cheek gave reason, if one were needed, for his fortifying himself with strong drink.

"And this villain had a pistol the size of a cannon, he did. And wavin' it around like, and that female shoved me out of the seat—"

A jokester in his audience said, "Probably you were trying to have it off with her—sure there was a highwayman?"

"She ran off with the rig, did she. And left me lying in my gore on the side of the road. She's a one, she is. No wonder the master got rid of her. A regular hellcat!"

A dissenter standing nearby objected. "No word about a highwayman in these parts. I dunno."

"I tell you that's what happened! He had a mask on! Just like that fella Turpin."

"Turpin! He was hanged in my grandfer's time!"

"I didn't say he *was* Turpin," cried the beleaguered groom. "I said he was *masked*, didn't I?"

"Never heard Turpin work a mask. A wig, I suppose. But what happened to your highwayman, Goff?"

"I dunno." Goff turned sulky, doubtless from a clear idea of the cowardly display he had made. "He was gone afore I come to."

While not precisely the case, Goff did not wish to reveal the depth of his suspicions, at least to this group. He too had seen the ring, not at the time of the holdup itself, but later, watching the highwayman rock in great pain over his cut face, his hands held up to ease his suffering. Having seen the ring, Goff had promptly fallen to the ground again, feigning unconsciousness, and after the master was safely on his way back to the house, he himself had come to the inn in search of comfort and, if possible, some trace of the horse and the curricle.

Marcus paid little heed to the group at the bar. The landlord, knowing quality when he saw it, provided him quickly with a private sitting room, a glass of brandy, and a promise of dinner to come.

Today had been uneventful. Tomorrow, in all likelihood, would be the same. Secure in his mistaken belief, Marcus North went in due course to his bed.

11

LOTTIE LOOKED over her shoulder, not for the first time since she had left the road for the plowed field. She saw no one following her. Probably Sir Albin had not yet recovered from the vicious blow she had struck with the whip.

One part of her mind was appalled at the violence she had just now committed, but another part—and this was the stronger—applauded heartily, and promised to do it again if occasion arose. Suddenly Miss Charlotte Forester found it hard to maintain her existence. Another creature seemed to have invaded her mind, a creature far more down to earth and, she began to suspect, one much more human than was a well-brought-up young lady sheltered from the world.

Of all things that dear Miss Wythe had prepared her for, the circumstance of trudging along the edge of a farmer's field, dirty from head to toe, not knowing where she would eat next, to say nothing of being certain of a place to sleep—this circumstance was not one.

The enormity of the attack on her was too much to think about. In truth, Lottie had all she could manage simply to set one foot ahead of the other, without planning as much as five minutes ahead.

She was plodding along in the direction of the inn, which had been her destination at the start. The coach would of course be on its way to Alford before she could arrive. Indeed, she thought she had heard only

moments ago the long sweet call of the horn signaling
the arrival of the stage. The inn must be closer than she
thought! She remembered that only one southbound
coach a day stopped at the inn, so if she planned to
travel to Alford, she would have nearly a day to spend—
somewhere.

She was so tired—tired and thirsty. She would give all
her possessions, she thought, for a restoring cup of hot
tea. She came upon a tree which cast welcome shade on
the ground, and heedless of soiling her gown, she sank
to the ground beneath it.

Soiling her gown! Her gown was already filthy at the
hem, streaked across the skirt, torn at the sleeve. All her
possessions for a cup of tea? She had no possessions at
all, save for the ragged clothes she wore, and a handful
of coins knotted in her kerchief.

Her situation was desperate.

Her pursuer, wounded and vindictive, behind her . . .
the coach gone until tomorrow . . . and the sun sliding
down the western sky. Lottie did the only thing possible.
She burst into tears.

Surprising as it seemed, Lottie realized that her bout
of crying settled her nerves and gave a focus to her
mind. She must make a plan, and that at once. Every
moment of delay, she was sure, would inflame the
temper of Sir Albin. He was as unpredictable as a
March wind, and as cruel, and she must be out of his
reach before he came after her.

But where should she go?

Into her mind crept the thought that had come to her
recently, one that she had spurned even when she was
troubled at Pentstable, before her flight to Alford.

Now she realized once more that her only hope lay
again in flight—a knowledge that she had had from the
beginning, when Lady Monteagle's letters lay between
her and her mother on the breakfast table.

Flight only as far as Alford—that was what she had planned. But circumstances had conspired against her, and she had traveled farther north on Miss Wythe's behalf.

Now it seemed so clear to Lottie that she could not understand how she could have been so blind as not to see it before. Her goal must be, and perhaps in the recesses of her mind had always been, Pomfret Priory.

Very well. Now that she understood that, she would go. North to Pomfret, even though she did not know how far it was, nor precisely how to get there. But two things she knew: Pomfret lay to the north, and she must leave Drysdale country as swiftly as though on wings.

She dared not wait for tomorrow's coach. Besides, it went south to Alford. She was not sure about the north-bound coach, even though she had traveled on it from Alford. At any rate, she was in no fit condition to board a stagecoach.

She sat in the welcome shade for a long time. When at last she rose, feeling an ache in every joint from her hard walking—it was clear she had not recently had sufficient exercise!—her plan was far from complete. However, her confidence rose with the certainty that Pomfret lay ahead, and somehow she would get there.

One cheering thought went with her as she set out again. She was not "Miss Wythe," with a reputation to uphold. Nor was she Miss Charlotte Forester, a young lady of impeccable behavior, sought in marriage by a stranger. She was free—a female without a name, at least one she would vouchsafe to anyone for the moment, and without supervision either by governess, or mother, or the dowagers of London society.

In truth, for the first time in her life, Lottie was . . . Lottie!

Moving cautiously, but as swiftly as she could, since it would soon be twilight, she approached the inn from the

rear. The building lay in a hollow, surrounded by
shrubbery, providing some kind of cover as she inched
forward.

She came to a halt in the shadow of a large bush and
examined the scene that lay before her. She was at the
back of the stable building. Beyond lay the inn itself.
Already there were lamps lit in two of the upstairs
rooms. The inn would be crowded this night. All the
better for her purposes. The servants would be too busy
to keep careful watch outside.

Her sight was good, and she could see that although
the coach had gone on its way, trying to make the next
town before darkness fell, there was still much activity
in the innyard. A handsome curricle stood by the far
wall, giving her a start at first, until she realized it was
not the Drysdale curricle. She spared a moment to
wonder what had happened to the horse she had tied up
in the woods. Surely by now he would have taken
action, broken the limb, and returned, she hoped, to his
own stable. At any rate, she did not see it here in the
innyard.

Not only her sight but also her sense of smell was
good. Too good—she wrinkled up her nose at the
pungent odor that wafted her way from the stable. If
she had been set down blindfolded in the wilderness of
Arabia Felix—the orange spot on Delia's globe—she
would have recognized that a stable, fully occupied,
stood near at hand. The aroma of kitchen discards, wet
straw, manure, bran mash, was unmistakable.

She waited. No one came. From time to time a door
slammed in the inn, but no sound came from the stables
save an occasional hoof pawing the dirt floor.

She had never felt so alone in her life.

Knowing that if she stayed where she was, she might
well put down roots, she darted quickly toward the
stable, and in a moment was inside.

She was enveloped in sudden gloom. The odor inside

the building was less strong, and the acrid aura of horse predominated.

Her eyes grew accustomed to the dimness, and she could make out the hulking shapes of stalled horses, bins along the walls to store feed, tack hanging on hooks on the walls. At least she was not out in the open, vulnerable to anyone in the innyard who might turn his head her way. But she was still far from safe, for if anyone entered the stable, she would be caught like a rabbit in a snare, with no way to explain. She would be fortunate if she were not put away as a felon!

Spurred by necessity, as well as the sound of a voice near at hand and approaching, she sought shelter. Knowing stables well, she knew there must be a ladder up into the mow. There it was!

Hand over hand on the rungs, feet scrabbling for a foothold—her boots were nearly worn through from the long walk, and her feet burned—she swarmed up the ladder into the mow. At last she was safe. Unless, of course, she thought, someone decided to come up with a pitchfork to send hay down below for the horses.

But the voice from outside, one ostler talking to another, she surmised, did not come any closer. She stayed where she was without moving. The hay was soft to lie on, and she was reminded of the many naps she had taken on sunny summer afternoons in the mows of Pentstable. Those were happy days, as she looked back, although she could not remember much enjoying them at the time.

Now all that was behind her, and she could not see into the future. Tonight was the only time she could be sure of. She wished she had had the foresight to pack a lunch before she left Drysdale. But if she had been possessed of clairvoyance, she would never have come to the Drysdales in the first place.

Hungry she was, and lonely, but she was warm enough in the haymow, and in the midst of imagining her situation had she not escaped once again from the villainous Sir Albin, she fell asleep.

She woke to daylight, and bewilderment. Where was she? And what was she doing here sleeping in her clothes? She turned her head, feeling a wisp of hay tickle her ear. More mystery. Her gaze fell upon a thin shaft of sunlight slanting in through a crack in the side of the building, where a pair of boards did not quite match. The ray of light was filled with dancing motes of dust, and she knew with a rush where she was. It took a moment longer to remember just why she had been forced to shelter in this place.

One regret she had. Only one? . . . Well, she added to herself, one of many. She wished she had her trunk. But the trunk lay in the road to Drysdale House, unless it had already been picked up. At any rate, the trunk would doubtless be forwarded to its real owner, "Miss D. Wythe, Alford." What would Miss Wythe make of her trunk returning without Lottie, or any word from the vanished Miss Forester? Lottie could not imagine. But she would think about that on another occasion.

Just now, on her hands and knees she scrambled to the wall and found a knothole to give her a view of her surroundings. She was looking into the innyard. There were several farm wagons, as well as that stylish curricle. The farm wagons caught her fancy. If she were to get a ride on one, heading north of course, she would be safe from pursuit either by Sir Albin or by the bailiffs or whatever law officers might be delegated to find her.

But in her present state, who would offer her a ride?

Below her, a groom came out to tend to his cattle, an ostler with him. Lottie withdrew into the silence of the hay and waited.

Eventually she was rewarded. A golden opportunity offered itself, and swiftly she slid down from the haymow. Quickly she took the ostler's clothing hanging on a nail in the wall. Had the garments been there the night before? It was entirely possible, but it had been too dark to see.

Now dressed in a nameless mucky nether garment topped by a scarcely cleaner smock, Lottie hesitated, the ostler's greasy cap in her hands. With a sigh she decided there was nothing else for it, so she clapped it on her head, tucked up her mass of hair under it, and pulled down the bill to hide the white streak in her hair.

She wished she had a mirror. On the other hand, perhaps it was better so. She might well be disgusted with her appearance. She looked down at herself. There had been times in the past when she had bewailed her lack of curves. Now was not one of them. She could pass easily for a boy, she thought, at least long enough to get right away from this district. Carrying her discarded clothes in her hand, she tiptoed to the door. It was time to leave. One last glance around the stable brought her to a halt. Surely that could not be food? She turned avidly to look. It was indeed food! The ostler's breakfast, bread and a bit of cheese, that he had set down when he was summoned from the inn.

In a trice the bread and cheese vanished from the low shelf, and Lottie from the stable.

Not until she had made a wide circle into ways unseen from the inn, always trending north, did she deem herself secure. She tucked the rags she had worn into a crevice between a couple of rocks, and found a bush under which she could sit. Then she fell upon the food she had stolen.

Licking the last crumb from her finger, she sighed hugely. Now she felt better. Now she could really think about what to do next. And now she knew no more than she had before. She must go north in the direction of Pomfret. Her best way was to cut the road north at a point far distant from the inn, and hope to pick up a ride on a farmer's wagon. She knew that even if the hue and cry had been raised, she was no longer recognizable as either Miss Forester or Miss Wythe. She sniffed the air. Neither by sight nor smell could anyone mistake her for anything but a lowly farm worker.

She had no idea how far Pomfret was, but she was not getting there while she sat under a bush. She got to her feet and set out.

At the moment, Sir Albin Drysdale was not in hot pursuit of the outrageous "Miss Wythe." Totally stunned by the failure of his ambush, and set raving by the excruciating pain of the whip across his face, he suffered from vanity wounded deeply. He could not believe he had been bested—not once, but twice!—by an ungrateful female. Ungrateful, he believed, because it could only be an honor to be seduced by a man with a title.

The mask he had worn in the guise of a highwayman had protected him from the worst of the damage. The mark of the whip was red, of course, but the skin was not broken in more than three places, and those would heal quickly. The agony he felt as he sat rocking in the road, hearing the hoofbeats and the sound of wheels receding swiftly into the distance, was that of a small spoiled child deprived of a bauble he wanted. Albin, of course, would not have recognized that explanation.

Finally pulling himself to his feet, knowing Lottie was beyond his present reach, he ignored Goff, the groom, lying apparently unconscious in the road, and staggered back to where he had tied his riding horse. Fury drove him to the house.

He would have a few things to say to that stupid groom when he returned. Why had he abandoned the curricle? Why had he not come to his master's assistance? Sometime later, he remembered that the groom had no way of knowing who the highwayman was, and he dared not give himself away. He had known one or two servants, not his, fortunately, who had tried it on when their master was discovered to be acting beyond the law. Not that he would have suffered such extortion himself, but it did pay to be careful.

But while he nursed his wound, the servants of Drysdale manor walked softly. To his disgust, even his stepmother seemed unusually elusive, almost as though she were avoiding him. Another mark against her—but she could wait. What could not wait, what must be attended to the very moment he could bare his face in public again, was the "education" of precious Miss Wythe.

The trunk, retrieved from the ditch where it had landed when jolted off the curricle, had been forwarded quietly to the address on the label. When Albin learned the baggage was out of his reach, he made short shrift of the coachman's protests and winkled Miss Wythe's address out of him.

Now, thought Albin, here is where I track down Miss Propriety! If she came from Alford, then it is a sure thing that she did not return there. She is not stupid, and she would know I would not let her get away with making me look the fool.

Therefore, I shall look for her in the opposite direction. When I find her, gloated Albin in the privacy of his own room, I shall take pleasure in overpowering her and teaching her a lesson she will never forget!

He brooded over the details of his revenge, until the picture was clear and very satisfactory in his mind. She'd never forget it!

But now he added: Supposing she survived it.

12

HOW MUCH brighter the day was, thought Lottie, now that she had eaten the ostler's bread and cheese. The sky was a soft blue overhead, decorated with small fat clouds driving from west to east.

Birds sang in the hedges, and far ahead a hawk circled over a field, watching, no doubt, for small scurrying animals to catch his eye.

It was, in fact, a day that a poet might sing of. Lottie had no words, nor, to be truthful, did she have sufficient breath to waste in talking to herself. She did not know how far she had to go, nor how many days she might be on the road.

If she could get a ride on a farmer's wagon, and then another, she might be at Pomfret before she knew it. Then, of course, she must introduce herself to the elderly Granville cousin—probably with much difficulty, Lottie thought, laughing as she looked down at her dreadful disguise. Fortunately, the breeze was steady, and the aromatic aura around the clothes was quickly dispelled.

Her boots were her own. Nearly worn through, yet they would serve for some time yet, and she had not had to "borrow" the clogs that had stood beneath the clothes she had taken. She would someday send money back to the inn for repaying the owner of the clothes she wore, but not yet. She had a few coins, but not enough even to take the stage north, supposing she were able to find decent clothes, some baggage, and even an abigail to make her appear respectable.

Respectable—that was a word, she realized practically, that was not remotely relevant now.

She shuddered to think what her mother would say, could that lady see her eldest daughter now. Even Miss Wythe, who knew more of the truth, would cluck in disapproval. Suddenly Lottie resented them all. Had it not been for them, she would be at home in Pentstable, riding Copper across the familiar fields instead of trduging on an endless treadmill of a road without any clear notion of her destination. It was not her own fault.

Her mother had been determined to force her into an unwanted betrothal, something like selling cattle at the local fair. Mr. North wanted only her estate, and even Miss Wythe was willing to take advantage of the situation to safeguard her own livelihood.

Not Lottie's fault at all!

The road blurred before her. Even the handful of sheep that looked at her over the hedge from their field seemed unaccountably woolly, until she realized that tears had risen in her eyes, unbidden, and overflowed down her cheeks. She blinked fiercely, and the stupid, kind faces of the sheep came into focus.

She could not believe that no wagon had come along. She had surely been traveling for hours, even though the sun seemed not to have moved across the sky. What had happened to all those vehicles in the innyard?

For the first time the thought occured to her: I might have to give up and beg a ride to Pentstable, or at least to Alford. Where else can I go for help?

But she would not give in—not yet. She had just begun to travel!

She rested several times, and saw with misgivings that the sun had crossed the zenith. The shadow on her right hand was lengthening perceptibly. Early afternoon already!

And then she heard the wheels. Someone was coming!

She looked back, eager to catch the first sight of her rescuer. She was much aware of her burning feet. The boots, made of leather soft as butter by a notable boot-maker, were never intended to march up and down the roadways of England.

She lifted one foot and then the other to rub most of the dirt from the toes. Suddenly conscious of her bedraggled appearance, she feared that no one would give her a ride even to the next town.

The desperation of her situation dawned on her. Whether she had been too exhausted before, or whether her life to this point had been too sheltered, it was hard to determine why she had not been sufficiently realistic before.

Now realism came to her with the force of a tidal surge. She was alone, unprotected, dirty, nearly destitute, with no friends near enough to succor her. Besides that, no one knew where she was, not even Miss Wythe.

But there was one man who might well guess the direction in which she was heading, one man who had reason to fear whatever disclosures she might make—a man whose mind she believed was obsessed with the desire for revenge, as well as with a desperate need to silence her!

The oncoming vehicle was still hidden from Lottie's view around the bend she had traversed just before hearing the approach of wheels. Whether it was her own lively suspicions, or whether the contour of the road, bending as it did around copses of trees—as though taking advantage of all the opportunities for ambushes —she did not know. But suddenly she realized that the sound of the wheels following behind her, and now very close to catching up to her, indicated a vehicle of style, of elegance, even of daintiness. Certainly no farm cart ever traveled with such lightness!

The approaching vehicle was a curricle, if she knew anything at all about vehicles, and moreover, one traveling smartly behind a pair of horses. Sir Albin! It *must* be Sir Albin coming along behind her, in hot pursuit. She could almost see his injured face, the furiously red line of the whip mark she had left on his face, the scarlet cheeks boding no good for his prey . . .

She looked wildly around her for shelter. No building. Even the trees behind her were mere saplings, able to shelter not even one as slender as she was.

There was only one thing to do, and she did it.

She dived into the ditch promptly, praying as she scrambled to get out of sight that there were no slugs in the stagnant water at the bottom of the ditch. Snakes she could deal with; slugs she could not.

The sound of the wheels, from her vantage point at this moment, were muffled by the earth that protected her. A low rumbling came to her, and the smart clop-clop of the pair moving briskly along the hard dirt road. She had covered her face with her hands as she scurried for cover, and now was conscious primarily of the stiff grass tickling her nostrils. She dared not sneeze.

Concentrating on controlling the sneeze, she was less aware of the wheels. She waited, however, until they had gone past her without, as she supposed, taking any notice of her. Her hiding place had served her well, the tall grasses covering her head, and the borrowed garments much more suitable than her light gray traveling gown would have been. The ostler's garb had either started out the color of mud or had acquired a stiff coating of dirt during its recent wear.

Besides the obnoxious grass tempting her to convulsive sneezing, she was also aware, as she had not been in the open air, that her clothing gave off an effulgence of its own, and one far from pleasant. She thought that even Sir Albin would spurn her now. Except, her realistic mind told her, for the revenge that, knowing Sir Albin even so slightly, she knew was part of the man.

At length, being sure that the curricle had gone on, since she could no longer hear the wheels, she gave way to the tickle in her nose and sneezed, a great convulsion of some force from its having been repressed for some moments.

She rose to her hands and knees, thankful to have escaped whoever it was in the curricle. Her confidence in her ability to make her way all the distance to Pomfret Priory, about which she had an imperfect idea, soared. She had outwitted the Drysdales so far, both by changing clothes in the stable and now by crouching in that dreadful ditch! She gave way to a momentary feeling of self-satisfaction.

If only she weren't so hungry!

A voice spoke over her head. ''What is it? Are you ill?''

Her heart sank to the bottom of her walking boots. She did not dare to look up. But she realized in a moment that the voice was not Sir Albin's. The curricle wheels must have been misleading—why did Scripture return to her in such an awkward moment? ''The hands are the hands of Esau, but the voice . . .''

She pushed herself up to her knees, and then to her feet. She could do nothing else, for there was a certain authority in the pleasant voice, and she suspected that the man would not go away until she answered. A masculine face, not unhandsome, looked down at her. The stranger's eyes held real concern, and she was moved.

''Are you ill?'' he repeated. ''Young man, let me help you out of that ditch. I am persuaded you have fallen badly. Are you injured?''

The voice and the words were those of a gentleman. His hand was stretched down to her, but her instinct served her well. She dared not place her soft fingers within his, and still maintain she was a country widow.

She shook her head, and in a moment climbed up to stand beside the man on the road.

The curricle, attended by a groom holding the heads of the pair, stood a few yards beyond.

"Where are you going?" said the stranger.

She gestured vaguely in the direction ahead, and the man smiled kindly. "No need, young man, to be afraid of me. Speak up. I am going north on this road, and you are welcome to ride as far as suits you."

He motioned Lottie toward the vehicle, and took a step forward. For the first time, the fitful wind brought an unwelcome aroma to his attention. Stables, he thought—also ditch, he added thoughtfully—and there was a strong suggestion of honest sweat.

"Up at the back," the stranger said hastily.

Irving, the groom, allowed himself to frown, but being a loyal servant of a good master, he said nothing. Maybe the speed of their progress down the road would provide sufficient breeze to send this ugly smell away behind them!

But what possessed the master to pick up a ragamuffin out of a ditch, he would never know. The master had been fitful in his mind, although always considerate, ever since that foray into the country—the jaunt that had turned out so badly for him. The young miss had, according to that footman, simply taken to her heels when the master drove up to the door of Pentstable. A foolish miss, to Irving's mind, for she could do a lot worse than take the master as a husband!

Marcus North, having provided the country lad found in a ditch with succor, dropped the boy from his mind and returned to his thoughts, gloomy enough at best.

Sustaining a disastrous blow to his self-esteem, never very high, by the defection of a young lady he had never seen, nor—more to the point—who had ever met *him*, he had thought to divert himself in the gaiety of a London Season winding down for the summer. Such relief, however, had not come his way.

Instead, he could now see that in his lonely misery he had forgotten to be wary. Annabella and her mama had very nearly captured him. Her mother, for one, had considered the match already made. He was a Bartholomew baby, he thought now, not wary enough to protect himself.

Marriage, previously much on his mind, now receded in a fog of self-recrimination. If Geoffrey had failed, then it was all too likely that Marcus would fail. That was why, with little fanfare, he had left London behind. Annabella might even now be wondering where he was, since he had not made her privy to his departure. If he had only thought then, he could have made himself secure by the smallest of lies. He could have pleaded an emergency at his estate, and—if he had had his wits about him!—could have suggested that his very solvency was in question. That would certainly have prevented any misunderstandings.

If he could not do himself any good by finding a wife, his thoughts keeping uncomfortable time with the rhythm of the eight hooves ahead of him, he might as well keep his estate affairs in order. He tried to fix his mind on various improvements in his livestock, and in the winter crops, but for a reason he did not quite understand, he found himself dwelling on the scene at the inn behind him this morning.

If he had thought the turmoil of the coach departing just as he arrived the afternoon before, the stage driver intent upon gaining another ten miles toward London before stopping for the night, had been a kind of controlled but riotous chaos, the scene this morning was, although in a different way, as confusing.

Overnight, it seemed, several inexplicable events had come to light. The highwayman's assault on a private vehicle, on its way to meet the coacch, had not gone unnoticed. Comment ranged from "What is the world coming to?" all the way to "What happened to the passenger?"

The passenger was, variously, Lady Drysdale's elderly mother (until someone mentioned she had been dead for ten years), a chambermaid caught with a handful of Lady Drysdale's jewels, and a light-o'-love of Sir Albin's, dismissed to make her own way back to the city.

One thing that all the commentators agreed on: there was no sign of the passenger and therefore she must have been carried off by the highwayman for his own nefarious purposes. Not one of those in the inn, no matter how vocally indignant at the dastardly crime, had expressed any inclination to go to her rescue.

Although that episode seemed to have been forgotten by the local inhabitants this morning, yet life at the inn did not settle at once into its usual prosaic routine. There was something about a stableboy who had mysteriously done away with his clothes, and the unfortunate lad was clearly expecting punishment for his carelessness.

This lad he had picked up, Marcus realized, was surely connected with a stable somewhere, for the boy reeked of that unmistakable fragrance. But this boy clearly was in possession of his own clothes. No one, unless he were desperate, would stoop to steal such a redolent wardrobe!

13

WHILE LOTTIE wound her tentative way north in the general direction of Pomfret Priory, her trunk, forgotten both by its owner and by its borrower, had been sent swiftly on its own way by the sympathetic Drysdale staff. Thinking it likely that Sir Albin might well decide from pure malice to retain possession of the governess's property, simply to enjoy knowing she would be inconvenienced without it, several of the servants went out to search the road.

The trunk, bearing on its lid its owner's name and address in uncompromising letters, was hoisted onto a farm cart the day after it had fallen from the fleeing vehicle and taken to the coaching inn. In due course, it was lifted onto the roof of the coach and deposited at the station in Alford.

From there, by the kindness of a drayman who knew Miss Wythe, it was delivered at last to its owner.

"Then," she said to the drayman, "Miss . . . that is, was there a young lady with the trunk?"

"No, miss. Nothing was said about a young lady. And I can tell you for sure that no one got off the coach in connection, you might say, with this trunk. But since it had your name on it, miss, I thought it best to bring it along."

"Of course," said Miss Wythe hastily, "you did very well, Thomas." She found a small coin to put into the hand ready to receive it, and, closing the door to ensure privacy, went into her small sitting room and regarded the wayward trunk.

There it was, her trunk. She had last seen it when it had left her house containing Lottie's new clothes, especially chosen for the unassuming life of a governess. She had heard from Lottie only in a brief note, assuring her that she had arrived safely and had settled in. But there was no other letter, and truly one could not have expected a Miss D. Wythe to write frequently from Drysdale House to a Miss D. Wythe in Alford.

Vexed with herself, Miss Wythe clucked and shook her head. She should really have thought a bit further ahead. She could easily have made arrangements for some means of communication so that she could hear how her dear Lottie was getting on. She could only lay the blame for such havey-cavey arrangements on the illness she had suffered then.

It was surprising how swiftly, once the matter of the Drysdale position had been solved, Miss Wythe had recovered her strength. Truly, she was not well enough yet to climb into a stagecoach and go to the Drysdales' herself to inquire about Lottie.

How could she inquire, even so? She might well interfere in plans Lottie had made in recent days, and spoil the lot for her.

But yet, the trunk sat there before her eyes, accusing her of she knew not what. But there must be something it had to tell her.

"Where is Lottie?" she demanded of the inanimate object. "Why did you come back here alone? If she went someplace else, why would she not take her trunk —*my* trunk, of course—with her?"

The trunk, as could have been expected, did not answer. The only thing, then, was to open it. Fortunately, the trunk had come with duplicate keys. After a frantic search, she found the spare key. The drop from the curricle as Lottie drove it like a Roman chariot down the road, an event of which Miss Wythe happily remained ignorant, had not sprung the lock or the hinges. Sturdily made, it gave no hint to its owner of its recent adventures, save for the dent on one corner.

Inside the trunk, somewhat jumbled to be sure, were packed Lottie's "governess" clothes. Miss Wythe had supervised every garment of that wardrobe, and she knew now just what was missing—one garment only, a lightweight muslin in a neutral gray.

That, then, must be what Lottie was wearing at the moment. However, it was just as well that, at that moment, Miss Wythe was not privileged to see her one-time student sitting on the curricle seat beside a Mr. Marcus North of Gresham Manor, Lottie still dressed in her ostler's garb, imperfectly cleaned in a reeking pond some little distance from the inn where they had stayed the night—separately of course, and the gentleman not knowing where his recent passenger had gone.

But the trunk held yet another surprise for Miss Wythe. At the bottom, carefully packed, was a small store of coins, wrapped carefully in a handkerchief secured by a knot. Counting it, Miss Wythe realized that she held in her hand the entire salary for the weeks that Lottie had been at the Drysdales'.

Plus, she calculated with a frown, an extra week's wages. As a bonus for the good job done? Or as a sop to a discharged employee?

Miss Wythe drew a deep and troubled breath. Culpable as she had been in soliciting Lottie's offer to take up the Drysdale position for her, she could now reflect that she had at least persuaded Lottie to write to her mother to say she was with Miss Wythe at Alford.

She herself had written again after a fortnight, wounding her conscience as little as possible by telling Lady Forester that Lottie was well but would remain in

Alford for a further visit. At least as far as Miss Wythe
had known at the time, Lottie was well.

Now, of course, she experienced the gravest doubts as
to Lottie's well-being, to say nothing of her safety. She
had not come back to Alford, the job finished for some
reason, with her trunk. Lottie was apparently somewhere in the wilds of Leicestershire clad in a gray muslin
gown.

Miss Wythe saw her duty clearly, if reluctantly. She
began to frame the words she would write this very hour
to Lady Forester at Pentstable.

Lady Forester had, in the past few weeks, been of two
minds about her eldest daughter. For one, she believed
that life at Pentstable, unruffled as it was since all the
remaining Foresters were of one opinion as to the
importance of Caroline's coming sojourn in London,
was much easier. On the other hand, however, she
began to realize for the first time how much a part of the
household Lottie had been. She had taken much of the
domestic management off her mother's shoulders, she
had been dutiful and reliable, and in every way but one,
most biddable.

Lady Forester applauded the girl's good sense in
taking temporary refuge with Miss Wythe in Alford,
even while regretting the headstrong determination that
had caused her to run away.

When Miss Wythe's first letter arrived, informing her
that Lottie would be staying on for some time, Lady
Forester was to a degree relieved. Now she could get on
with the preparations for Carrie's descent upon
London, without the prickings of what she recognized
as a guilty conscience. Her eldest daughter had not
received her due, that was certain.

However, to Lady Forester's own surprise, she discovered that she had a more than superficial affection

for Lottie. She knew, as she had known for some time, that it was Lottie's physical resemblance to the dowager Lady Forester that had set her so against the child when she was young.

Not only Lottie's appearance but also her very disposition worked against her. The dowager had been fond of her own way, had carried on quite as though she were not the plainest creature God ever made. Indeed, there were times when the dowager had acted as though she had been a famous belle, a diamond of the first water, indeed, a *great catch*. And perhaps she had been, although Lidia Forester's memories were less flattering, perhaps because more intimate.

And yet, taken feature by feature, attribute by attribute, the dowager had been nothing exceptional. Since the present Lady Forester had indeed been a beauty, the secret of the dowager's great social success had eluded her, and subsequently she was moved to consider that success as being nonexistent save in the old lady's mind.

It was sheer jealousy, as any observer might have noticed, but Lady Forester had never considered such an explanation.

But now she discovered that she missed Lottie. She had been too hard on the girl. She should not have insisted so uncompromisingly that Lottie meet the North man. An easier, more diplomatic approach would have been better, but so astonished had she been by Lady Monteagle's overtures that she had dealt badly with Lottie, mentioning an offer before she had even met him. Truth to tell, Lady Forester had feared that when he got a look at Lottie he might shy off. She could not pretend that Lottie would be an instantaneous success, no matter how well-disposed her suitor might be. Well, that scheme had not turned out at all well, but at least Lottie had come to no harm.

* * *

Lady Forester had much higher hopes of Carrie. A beauty like herself, and the most beguiling feminine ways! No matter that the girl was somewhat selfish. Where was the woman of sense who did not see to her own advantage wherever possible?

No, she had not handled Lottie well. But after Carrie was settled, then she, Lady Forester, would make it all up to Lottie. In the meantime, the girl was safe enough with that dowdy Miss Wythe. She could come to no harm there, and it was a relief not to have her underfoot, still sulking over her mother's efforts to see her settled!

Miss Wythe's second letter, fraught with unwelcome news and puzzling details, put an end to Lady Forester's complacency.

"I do not understand all this rigmarole about governesses and injured limbs and missing trunks," cried Lady Forester in bewilderment. Her only audience was Tyson, pouring the afternoon chocolate for his mistress. He stood, arrested, waiting for further confidences. He had been long years in Lady Forester's employ, and knew that, since she had no one else to talk to, she would soon inform him of what was on her mind.

A letter from Miss Wythe; Tyson knew that much. And the matter of it disturbing to the mistress, and, without a doubt, to do with Miss Lottie. The butler held his breath.

"Why would Miss Lottie take a job—one that belonged to Miss Wythe in the first place? What does that woman mean—the trunk arrived alone? Arrived from where? And I suppose the trunk did not leap to the coach roof and ask to be tied down? The woman is daft! And where is Lottie? I should have discharged that woman long since!" Ignoring the fact that she had indeed discharged Miss Wythe since Carrie could not abide her, and that she had regretted that action frequently, she turned to Tyson. "What do you make of it?"

"I could not say, my lady," said Tyson, hiding his eagerness to read the missive, "since I have not perused the letter."

"Here. See what you think."

She tossed the letter into his ready hands, and watched his face. His expression turned blank, a sure sign that he was worried.

"I thought so," she said. "Now what shall we do?"

Tyson, dissuaded from his first suggestion—that he, along with a pair of stout footmen, should travel post-haste to the Leicestershire seat of the villainous Drysdales—at length put his mind to assisting Lady Forester frame the phrases to be addressed to the unknown Lady Drysdale, seeking information about her daughter's governess, under whatever name she had passed. "Waiting, my lady, will be the most difficult thing for you," said Tyson. His mind full of dire conjectures as to what might already have befallen a gently nurtured young lady alone and unprotected, he added on a gloomy note, "It will be for all of us."

The gently nurtured young lady was not alone.

That morning she had left the inn stable where she had spent the night, again in a friendly haymow, and headed away from the buildings, always trending north. She had set her mind the night before, while she waited for sleep to come, to recalling the names of towns she remembered as having something to do with Pomfret.

North, she knew. Derbyshire, she knew. But what town might be the northernmost point on this road, the town where she must turn west to find Pomfret, she was not sure.

Certainly she needed to have some goal in mind to shape her further journey. At length, remembering her dear grandmother's tales about her childhood at

Pomfret Priory, one name sprang into her mind. Castleton! Grandmother had gone to assemblies at Castleton, danced the night away at Castleton, shopped for her elaborate trousseau in Castleton.

And to Castleton Lottie would go.

But progress would be very slow. On foot this morning, she could only regret that she had not in fact stolen the curricle that had been in her hands for a short time. Since Sir Albin would undoubtedly pursue her to exact his revenge on her for his wound, she might as well have taken the curricle to make his pursuit more difficult.

How different was the Lottie of Pentstable from the Lottie now trudging along the road like any hedgebird! What would Lady Monteagle think now if she could see Lidia Forester's girl marching down a dusty road—very hungry, and suffering from a peeling red nose—wearing ugly and smelly clothes?

The smartest thing she had ever done, she reflected, was to refuse even to meet Lady Monteagle's gentleman. She suspected darkly that, had she given in, the combined pressure of her mother and Lady Monteagle would have overwhelmed her. Since her mother had let slip that Mr. North's lands lay alongside Pomfret, Lottie was convinced he wanted only her property. It would not matter to him that she was plain. But oh! how it mattered to her!

Now the young gentleman who had plucked her out of the ditch yesterday lingered in her mind. He had been gentlemanly indeed, not even flinching when he caught the scent of her clothing. He had given her a long ride along the way, and even had suggested that she stay in the same inn with him, as a stableboy, of course. But she had dropped down from the back of the curricle before he could insist too much, and vanished from the road.

She had walked for more than an hour on this bright morning. The breeze of yesterday had picked up today, and in truth developed an unpleasant habit of buffeting her. She reached up to pull her hat further down on her head, shading her sunburned face from a further burn.

The gentleman and his groom came upon her before she was aware of them. The wind muffled the sound of their wheels, and she saw them too late to run.

Without a word, her rescuer pulled his pair neatly to a stop and motioned her to the boot.

With an independence inappropriate under the circumstances, she shook her head. Lowering her voice in an effort to sound boyish, she said, "No need to carry me on. I'll do fine."

She turned her back on the curricle and plodded on. She longed to ride. But she dared not. With Sir Albin's perfidy lively in her mind, she could not take a chance on this stranger. She believed she could trust him, but then, she had been mistaken before.

She heard the horses walking sedately up to overtake her, but she did not look up. If she refused to go with him, he could do nothing to her. She hunched her shoulders against him and went on.

Then it happened.

A gust of wind swirled around the horses beside her and caught her unaware. It lifted her cap, and in glee sent it flying toward the ditch.

And behind her she heard the gentleman speak. "Good God!" he exclaimed. "You're a . . . girl!"

Irving, the groom, dropped to the ground and rescued the cap. Eyeing his master for instructions, he nonetheless enjoyed the spectacle before him. The waif stood dejected in the road. An enormous mass of light auburn hair cascaded around her sagging shoulders, hair with a strange streak of white springing up from her forehead. Bereft of her shadowing cap, her eyes were fixed on Irving's master—great green eyes.

Irving, no sentimentalist, yet willed his master to take the young miss up at once. And Irving, for the life of him, did not know why he knew that the female, dressed as she was, dirty as though she had wallowed in a sty, alone on the road without attendants, was quality—but he knew it.

Marcus North, bemused by the transformation of a derelict wait into an unprotected female, finally stirred himself. Humor tinged his voice. "You don't need to be afraid of me," he told her, "and I can promise you Irving will behave himself."

Stung by injustice, Irving glared at his master.

"Are you running away?" Mr. North asked his erstwhile passenger. "Shall I find the Bow Street Runners after me?"

"Certainly not."

"Ah, I am pleased to note that you have abandoned that unattractive growl. Oh, I see that you were led to it."

"It really hurt my throat," Lottie confided.

More crisply he said, "What did you have to eat this morning?" When she did not answer, he continued. "Nothing, as I suspected. Very well, here is some bread and cheese for you. I am sorry to tell you that the napkin is stolen, for I did not wish to arouse the inn-keeper's suspicions by asking for a luncheon to take with me."

Her gaze shifted from his face to the packet he now held in his hand. She was hungry indeed. Never had she gone so long without food in her pampered life. It was *degrading* to be so hungry. She could not even be sure she would act properly, as a lady should!

"Come now," coaxed Marcus, reaching a hand down to her. "Best not to stand in the road. If you are indeed a fugitive, say a schoolgirl running away from her boarding school, then the headmistress may even now be hot upon your trail!"

With alacrity she took his hand and climbed up to the seat. No headmistress was following, but she could not say the same about Sir Albin Drysdale.

Her only remark before she fell upon the bread was, "I have money. I can pay you for this!"

His response was quick and firm. "You cannot pay me. Keep your money. You may have need of it, from what I conjecture to be your situation. I confess I am not much impressed by the financial prosperity I have seen you enjoying to date."

Irving, riding contentedly at the back, pondered this new development. His master had been blue-deviled in recent days, ever since their return to London, and the groom saw signs that the young miss might pull him out of his sulks.

Indeed, conversation between the two was going along merrily. The repast had restored Lottie to cheerful optimism, a state of mind sadly missing of late.

"So you will not tell me your name?" Marcus was saying. "I think you are wise. But look at this knotty problem from my point of view, if you will. I cannot continue to regard you as anonymous, can I?"

"I shall not object."

"Ah, but suppose your pursuers come upon us. How shall I know which name to deny, if I do not know which name is correct?"

"You are teasing me."

"You have no solution?"

"In such a situation as you suggest, the answer is quite simple. Deny them all."

He sensed that he was treading too closely upon her privacy. He fell silent for some minutes. That the girl was in trouble was obvious. His fancy of a pursuer was only partly in his imagination. Logic told him that only a compelling reason could account for her condition, her obvious intention to travel north, and—recalling her quick evasive dive into a ditch yesterday upon his approach—her fear of something or someone.

Remembering at last a recent excursion to the theater in London, he suggested, "I have hit upon a name that suits the situation. May I address you as Viola?"

To his surprise, she laughed aloud. "If you wish, I shall not object. But in return, pray do not introduce yourself to me as the Duke Orsino."

He was startled beyond belief. Not only was this discovery of his an appealing and—if he could once see her face washed—likely attractive girl, but she was also educated. He gave a passing thought to the lovely Annabella. She had been his companion at the theater on the occasion he remembered, and she had not been able to unravel even that simple plot.

"If you insist upon names," the girl beside him added, "I think Sebastian is most appropriate."

He grinned. Viola in the play had dressed like a boy to be close to her great love, the Duke Orsino. The character of Sebastian was Viola's brother.

While Marcus felt no premonitory stirrings in the region of his heart, yet it did not do one's self-esteem much good to be relegated at once to the status of brother.

But the girl was right. In such an unconventional situation, arm's-length was the only safeguard they had. If anyone of this girl's family—who were doubtless of some substance, to educate a daughter of the house so well—had any thought that she had traveled even a day or two in his company, with only a groom as chaperon, her reputation might well never recover. Nor, he added honestly, his own either.

"I shall answer promptly to the name Sebastian," he told her gravely.

14

SIR ALBIN, upon his return to the safety of his home, found that home as dull as ever, enlivened only by the arrival of Miss Wythe, the governess. He had not thought her pretty, since his standards of beauty had been formed in lower segments of London society. She was too flat, too plain. But, not to put too fine a point on it, he thought—she was at hand.

He expected his first overtures to be rebuffed. No female would risk her position out of hand. So, not in the least downcast, he set himself a small wager. How many advances would it take before she agreed to meet him away from the house?

He could teach her a thing or two that she never learned in those books! Another goal—a kind of side bet, as it were—with which he entertained himself was how many encounters, say, in the woods, would it require until she admitted him, in the small hours, to her room?

And, he thought, dreading the inevitable ennui to come, how soon would it be before she was begging him to favor her, long after her scant appeal had worn off and dalliance, at least with her, could not divert him?

Nonetheless, the campaign would beguile the time until he could safely return to London. Probably half a dozen encounters at the most, and no more than two episodes on the uncomfortable forest floor to accomplish the second goal.

The lady was not willing.

Before a fortnight had passed, he found that that resistance increased his determination to bring Miss Wythe to her knees. No longer was it a question of physical desire, but simply a determination to crush an opponent.

And still Miss Wythe did not capitulate.

Even the threat of force in the ambush he laid in the home woods had been ineffectual, thanks to that stupid mutt of Delia's. Nor had the holdup on the road served its purpose. Instead, his mirror showed him a thin red slash down the side of his face that might possibly leave a scar for life. He pondered the idea of translating the source of that scar, for the benefit of his London friends, into the punishment of an anguished husband.

But there was something to be done first. The chit who had wielded that whip with such deadly effect, and had driven away with his gig and his horse, leaving him weltering in his own blood, must be punished for her impertinence. How dared she resist? She was a mere governess, and so not to be considered as having any wishes of her own.

And now he held the first clue as to where he might find her.

He was at hand when Lady Forester's letter arrived. Lady Drysdale was shocked past caution. "Look here, Albin, Miss Wythe . . . that is, not Miss Wythe but—"

Albin, seeing that his stepmother was genuinely distressed, took the letter from her resisting fingers. "Let me see," he said. "I'll never made head or tail out of what you are trying to say."

He read the letter quickly, and then again more slowly. "So your governess was no such thing." He sneered. "Trust you to make a mull of it. But if she is really Miss Forester, then why was she here?"

"I never heard of a Miss Forester," said Lady Drysdale.

"I have," said Albin, "but I can't remember the connection."

The connection, however, was clear in his mind. Among his friends he counted several impecunious gentlemen requiring marriage to heiresses. In their own interests, these friends possessed exhaustive knowledge of eligible ladies of property. Miss Forester's name had arisen, but since she had never come to London for a Season, details about her were scant. However, since her person was not the concern, information about her property was readily available.

"Where do you think the wench has got to?" Albin demanded of his stepmother.

"I . . . I am sure I could not say."

"Could not? Or would not? Didn't she tell you where she was going when she left?"

"If you recall, Albin," said Lady Drysdale gently, "she had no time to tell me very much of anything. Such an abrupt, unkind thing to do—"

"Don't let's go over that again!" said Albin roughly. "She offended me, and she had to go."

Without so much as a thought about his stepsister's well being, or her own wishes, she thought, but did not say. However, she had learned, not easily, a valuable lesson—never to oppose him.

"She came from Alford," said Lady Drysdale helpfully, knowing that he was already aware of that. "So I suppose she went back, at least at the start."

Her stepson looked at her with contempt. "But she never got there. The letter said so. Can't you read?"

"I did not say," she said, "that she stayed in Alford. But where else would she go?"

"That's what I'm asking you. Did she ever mention Pomfret Priory? That property she is supposed to have, somewhere in the north, I believe?"

"No."

I thought he had never heard of her, thought Lady Drysdale to herself. I wish I had had the sense to hide this letter when I received it, except how could I know what was in it?

"If she didn't go back to Alford, and she didn't go back to her home, then . . ." It was clear to Albin that the elusive Miss Forester had set her sights on her own property in the north.

Well, that decision was just about going to finish the woman off. He would track her down, woo her gently, apologize—women always liked apologies when accompanied by trivial gifts!—marry her, and *then* she would learn what kind of man she had insulted!

The second evening of Albin's journey to the north brought him to a town of no size, but with a small inn. He traveled alone, without his groom. He was not sure what possibilities might present themselves when he caught up with Miss Forester, but he did not intend to be restrained by the presence of a watchful and probably disloyal servant.

Also, he had traveled in haste, since the chit had a good start on him. It had taken at least a day, he guessed, for the trunk to reach its real owner, another day to get the news of Lottie's disappearance to Lady Forester, and another day for Lady Forester's letter to reach his stepmother. There was much ground to cover, but Albin reasoned that she could not well travel alone, without an abigail, and avoid embarrassment or worse. Therefore she would not stay at the better-known inns, or those in larger towns.

Albin had no clear idea of the mechanics of public travel. Did one buy a ticket and climb upon the stage? Or would a bandbox be required? He could not believe she would set out for the north on foot, so she must be riding.

But in a public coach? Or a farm wagon? Did she purchase a horse, as he would himself, and ride on the York road like Dick Turpin?

Albin made frequent inquiries. Unfortunately for him, his questions, put for the most part in an arrogant manner, failed to elicit any useful information.

"A young woman," he demanded, "by herself—"

"'This is a respectable house, sir, and not wishing any discourtesy to quality, yet an unattended female has never stayed in this inn, nor will. If you get my meaning."

After the fifth set-down of this kind, Albin perceived that his task was not as easily accomplished as he had thought at the start.

Instead of turning back, as any reasonable man might do, he merely became more headstrong in his purpose. After all, he told himself, only bourgeois are required to be reasonable. Gentlemen, even those of only the second generation, were permitted their whims.

The inn where he pulled up late on the second day of his journey was no more prepossessing than the others he had stopped at. But the afternoon was wearing on, evening was approaching, and he had no wish to be benighted in this godforsaken land. Besides, if he were not mistaken, the weather was brewing up a storm. There would be rain before morning, and likely they were in for a week or more of it. He wished he had not decided to drive the curricle. Although the vehicle was excessively fast, it provided no substantial shelter from a steady rain.

He hoped that little Miss Forester had the same kind of weather-wise sense. He did not wish her to be caught out in a storm, not for any concern for her health or comfort, but simply because she would be harder to find.

Albin was reasonably confident that his strategy was sound. He would simply continue his questioning at the smaller inns, searching for the wayward Miss Forester, but if all else failed, he could run her to earth at Pomfret Priory. He was as sure of her destination as he was of his own name.

The innyard, when he arrived, was small, but at least there was a curricle of quality there, and a groom leading away the pair that had clearly brought the vehicle this far. Beside the groom trotted a small figure, dancing attendance on the groom. Some London dandy stopping here, no doubt, sporting his tiger as well as a more useful servant.

Albin found himself staring overlong at the scene. Was he simply admiring the prime cattle, as he believed, or was there something else? He could not be sure. Some odd quirk of memory, perhaps, doubtless the result of fatigue, for he had really been putting his own cattle along.

There was nothing at all familiar about the groom or the small boy beside him. How could there be? Albin had never been in this part of England before.

He had turned away, after tossing his reins to an ostler, and thus did not see the small boyish figure beside Marcus' groom turn to look long at the new-comer. So close was he, and yet so oblivious of his good luck!

The landlord was suitably impressed with his own good fortune. Two gentlemen arriving, separately, on the same evening! He rubbed his hands enthusiastically, mentally adding sums and raising prices. The first gentleman, a Mr. North, had paid well for the accommodation of his servants, both of them. The inn-keeper smiled broadly as the second just-arrived gentle-man came through the door.

There were gentlemen, he thought later, and then there were gentlemen. The second arrival was certainly not of the same quality as the first. The second had no sooner entered than he began his usual interrogation.

"I'm looking for a female—"

The innkeeper, already disenchanted with Sir Albin, said sourly, "I furnish only bed and victuals. No females."

"Blast your eyes!" cried Sir Albin with growing rage. "I don't need the likes of *you* to provide me with suitable companionship!" Then, suddenly realizing he was engaging in an unsuitable argument with a mere innkeeper, he stopped short. He added, "Another kind of female, I meant."

The inn host suggested, "A runaway?" His tone left no doubt that he sided with any runaway that Sir Albin pursued.

The inquirer had come to the end of his rehearsed questions without success. He was forced now to improvise. Not being a master of invention, he could only use what facts he possessed, and warp them slightly. "My young sister," he confided, "ran away from her governess, and my mother is quite distraught. Have you seen. . . ?"

Marcus North, descending the stairs from his bedroom at that moment, stopped short. He had not heard the first part of the argument, but it seemed clear that the two men had been conversing for some time. While he missed most of the pertinent details of Albin's quest, he took exception to the tone of voice in which he was pursuing it. He was to be here for only one night, however, and he could easily take steps to avoid the man for a few hours.

In the kitchen, with the rest of the servants, Irving and Lottie sat eating. The food was not exceptional, but Lottie was ravenous. She bent her head low over her plate, to keep her face in shadow and also to make listening to the conversation around her easier.

Always she had at the back of her mind that Sir Albin would not be satisfied until he had taken his revenge for the nasty cut she was sure she had inflicted on his face. The mask had kept her from seeing the extent of the damage her whip had done, but there had been no masking of the fury in the eyes behind the mask.

Albin was a vengeful man. Look at, for instance, the way he had insisted on her dismissal, solely to salve his hurt feelings.

But nonetheless it came with a shock to realize that he had indeed come after her, had seen her in the stable-yard. She could not be sure that he had recognized her, but of course she was equally uncertain that he had not.

Suddenly she pushed her plate back. She was not hungry anymore. Suppose Albin's groom came in to supper! She had not seen him, but then, she had averted her face so quickly that an army might have walked in and she not have known it. It was not Albin's custom, she was sure, to travel more than a league away from home without someone to see to his comforts. It did not occur to her that he would be riding alone.

His groom would know her. Her disguise would be penetrated. Her rescuer, whose name she did not know, might well be blamed for unknown sins . . .

Without a word, she fled into the night.

She had no clear plan of action. She sought only to avoid recognition. She moved sideways along the side of the building, where the eaves provided a little protection.

It would rain before morning, without doubt.

The moon had risen to a point in the heavens suitable for shedding a pale but illuminating glow over the countryside. The stable building was a huge dark hulk against the silvered meadows, and somewhere a stream gurgled softly. But there were far-off flashes of lightning in the depths of the clouds banked in the west, and she was enormously reluctant to give up the shelter that lay at hand.

She considered herself safe from Sir Albin, at least for tonight, and she would simply have to take to the road as early as possible, before anyone at the inn was stirring.

15

MARCUS KNEW nothing about his companion's change of plans. He felt restless, unsettled. The coming storm was still tucked into the bank of clouds in the west, and, countryman that he was, unsettled weather always had its effect on him. He realized that his uneasy thoughts were circling one focal point, rather like a pack of dogs suspiciously eyeing a stranger whose quality was not readily apparent.

This female who rode with him was the puzzle. He knew nothing about her. She had refused to tell him her name, and in kindness he had christened her for the moment Viola. Before that, however, she had striven to maintain the fiction that she was a stableboy, a tale whose proof her clothing sturdily provided.

Equally cautious, and perhaps still stinging from his belief that Annabella in London cared for his name and fortune rather more than for the man, he had not told this waif his name either, or where he lived, or even where he was going.

Left to his own uncomfortable thoughts in his private sitting room, he had nothing else to do but to let his mind play over the various possibilities that might lead "Viola" to take to the road in boy's clothing.

First, of course, was the manifest peril in which a lone female walked on the roads of England. It was all very well to talk about England being a bulwark of law and order, but that belief, when put to the test, failed in the main. Possibly England was safer than Venice or the darker streets in Naples, in both of which cities Marcus had spent some time.

But when it came to simple truth, a lone woman, of quality or of the lower classes, could not set out from one village in the sure hope of arriving unmolested at the next.

What teased his thoughts most, however, was the entirely unjustified feeling that Viola should have seen him for the trustworthy gentleman he was. He knew he would not force her to give in to his baser instincts, and, entirely illogical in the conclusion he came to, *she should have known that*!

Just how that knowledge should have come to her, he did not know. Nor did he attempt to discover just why her trust was so important to him.

He was thus not in the best of moods when his sitting room was abruptly invaded by the obnoxious stranger.

"I suppose you have commandeered the sitting room for yourself," the stranger began on a surly note. "It's the only one in this forsaken place, and I make sure you will have no objection to sharing it."

When Marcus made no answer, Sir Albin stepped farther into the room. He held a bottle in one hand. "We've a long stormy night ahead of us, and we may as well make the best of it." He waved the bottle above his head. "Not great, but the best Landlord has. And worth a pretty penny to him, although you may be sure I did not pay him what he asked. Stand firm, I always say, and they climb down off their high horse! Don't you agree?" Without waiting for Marcus' answer, he added, "The damned fool did not send in glasses, did he?"

Marcus, finding his own thoughts unpalatable, nonetheless did not welcome the intrusion. "As a matter of fact, I do not agree," he said, to his own surprise.

Ordinarily a tolerant man, he could explain his instantaneous dislike of this man only by remembering his inquiry about a young lady. Albin had so far gained caution enough not to ask for the wench by name, only by description.

"I should not have hired the parlor had I not wanted to be alone. I do object to your presence, sir."

It was unfortunate that Albin Drysdale had found no release for his belligerent nature for some weeks. Now, at last, was an opportunity he could not pass up.

"I told you," he said in a menacing tone he had frequently found useful, "that this is the only sitting room in the inn."

"Then may I suggest the stables," said Marcus, "as being a more suitable setting for your bad manners."

Words, however sharp, did not lead to blows. It was clear to Albin that the man facing him, who had slowly risen to his feet, was not to be easily intimidated. While not appearing at first to be of unusual fistic prowess, he would nonetheless strip to advantage at Jackson's. Sir Albin had no wish to put the matter of the sitting room to the test.

Albin Drysdale had not reached this stage in his life by wading into a mill without due consideration. This was not the man to back down. However, Albin decided, there were other ways of expressing his opinions, and at once a dastardly scheme unfolded before him.

He laughed, eyeing his opponent uneasily. "No need to get in a huff over nothing. Just wanted to share the brandy . . ."

Marcus was left to his unpalatable thoughts. The more he thought about Viola, the more he believed the girl was in real danger. Her disguise, her uncommunicative ways, above all a certain wary look over her shoulder from time to time—she was fleeing some kind of danger. Suddenly he became aware of a new sensation—he had developed a very strong protective sense. In only two days!

He must help her in whatever way he could. To start:

a set of Irving's clothes, too large and not delicate, but
clean! Perhaps he could stand guard while she washed.
And while that glorious hair of hers was a very fetching
color, if they went far together he might well insist that
Irving take the shears to it.

No, not Irving, he decided. He himself would see to
her transformation.

The inn was quiet. The stableyard was filled with
small equine sounds, and the moonlight shone brightly
enough to lure small night animals into the open.

As peaceful as the scene seemed from his window,
Marcus found no rest in it. The girl—Viola—was
unaware of the menace posed by the ill-bred stranger.
He was asking for a young lady, and while there was no
indication that Viola was the object of his inquiry,
equally there was no certainty that she was not.

Marcus discovered a deep-rooted objection to the
idea of Viola and that bumptious lout together for any
reason whatsoever. Suppose Viola, all unsuspecting,
were to emerge from her room in the morning and
descend into the presence of the stranger?

He must warn her. And while he was at it, he might
well effect the other alterations in her presence that had
occurred to him.

Fortunately he had been able to convince Viola that
she should sleep in the inn. Irving had taken the "lad"
with him as his assistant, seeing that she ate well in the
kitchen, and lodging her in a room adjoining his in the
attic. Marcus started in the direction of the attic stairs.
Halfway there, he paused, and then returned to his own
room.

That hair! In some obscure way, he set a test for
Viola. If she were honestly fleeing a tangible peril, as he
believed, she would be willing for the sake of her safety
to sacrifice that telltale cascade of hair that gave her

gender away at a glance. He took one of his own razors out of its case and climbed the stairs to the attic.

There were only two doors opening from the landing. From the one on the right came a sound of prodigious snores. Having heard them many times before, he knew that behind that door lay Irving, dead to the world.

He tapped lightly on the other door. Hearing no answer, he pushed the door slightly ajar and peeked in. The room was empty.

His first thought was anger. He had spent a good bit of the evening worrying about her, and had decided to come to her rescue, and she was not even here! He turned away. If she had so little regard for his wish that she sleep inside the inn for a change, then she was nothing to him. He would simply go back to his room, put the razor away, and leave her to her own devices. If she were indeed fleeing from the boor sleeping under this same roof, he could not help her. Particularly if she had already fled.

Suppose she had taken to her heels, avoiding that fellow? She was also avoiding Marcus, and that bruised his own self-esteem.

He hefted the razor in his hand. His mind was made up to leave her to her own devices, but his emotions remained unconvinced. He realized that within him a tender protectiveness was growing. He could not abandon her without a further effort to find her. He deliberately closed his mind to whatever he was feeling. He had some responsibility for the girl, after all. He had carried her this far, and without his help she would not have arrived so swiftly at this inn, just in time to meet this stranger asking about young ladies.

He could not believe she would start on a longer journey with the storm sure to strike before morning. Perhaps, in her usual way, she had gone to seek shelter in the stables.

He turned and entered Irving's room. One might well shoe horses in this room and Irving would not stir. Marcus emerged with Irving's spare clothing tucked under his arm, and, quietly descending the stairs, let himself out a side door.

Lottie was indeed in the stable, curled up miserably in the haymow. Sir Albin had caught up with her, and although she did not know just how, he was sure to find her. There was nothing for her to do but to wait for false dawn and set out again on the road. Trending north always, but that direction was no longer safe, not with Sir Albin successful in tracking her this far.

She was startled by the smallest possible noise below her. The horses were shut into boxed stalls, munching hay with vigor. This was quite another sound. She listened, holding her breath. The noise came again. There was someone below on the stable floor.

With infinite care she peeked over the edge of the mow. A door stood open, and the moonlight streamed in. The dark silhouette of a man stood just inside the door, in an obvious listening pose. He moved slightly, and the light struck an object in his hand and reflected from it.

The man had a razor!

She squealed, the merest squeak of a sound, but it was enough. The man looked up at her, and she recognized him. "Sebastian!" she breathed. "You frightened me to death!"

Abashed, he looked down at the razor in his hand. "Good God, no wonder. I'm sorry."

He moved closer to the mow, and—rather like Romeo and Juliet, she thought, herself in the balcony!—they held a whispered colloquy.

"Your hair," he said. "Do you not think it should be cut?"

She paused only a moment. She had already given the

possibility some thought, but she had no instrument. Now, here it was at hand. "Yes, I do. Will you lend me the razor?"

"No, you couldn't see to do it. Come on down."

"You mean, right now?"

"Of course. When else?"

Suddenly shy, she objected. "I truly need a bath. I am ashamed—"

"Nonsense!" he said roughly. "Get down here. I'll see to the bath!"

A note in his voice galvanized her. He was not a man to ignore, and if he said he wanted her to come to him, there was no question in her mind. She came down.

The next hour streamed by as in a dream. He guided her across what seemed to be a small field, until, to her surprise, they came to the bank of a small stream. "Now then, sit down where I can get at your hair." Obediently she sat down, and felt his knees at her back. He lifted her hair and said quietly, "You really want me to do this?"

Stifling her qualms, she said sturdily, "Yes, please."

Hearing the sharp crunch of the razor, she shut her eyes tightly and thought about something else, anything else. The job did not take long.

"Like Madame la Guillotine," she murmured. "What shall we do with . . . all that?" She gestured toward her fallen tresses.

"Leave them," he said briefly. "The local poachers will puzzle for months over what kind of beast was killed here."

To his relief, she giggled. She had made no real objection to cropping her hair. He began to feel respect for the courage with which she was facing the danger in which she believed herself to be. It was obviously a real and present peril.

"There," he said, "done. Not an expert job, but at least you won't give yourself away to the first stranger you see." After a moment he added, "You know that man at the inn was asking about a missing young lady?"

"Yes," she said softly. "I . . . I did not wish to meet him by chance, so I went to the stable. He'll never look there."

He waited. She clearly was acquainted in some strange way with the boorish stranger. Would she tell him? Did she trust him enough?

The answer was negative. She changed the subject. "Do you think that stream is deep?"

He sighed inwardly. She did not intend to confide in him.

"Let's look."

Together they found a pool deep enough to serve, and Marcus handed her the clothes he had borrowed from Irving. "Nothing fancy, I fear, but perhaps they will serve. They are at least clean."

She eyed the pool doubtfully. Part of it lay in shadow, but the larger part was silver in the moonlight. "Do you think tiddlers sleep?"

Amused, he said seriously, "Let us hope so."

Seeing her still hesitant, he reassured her. "I shall go to that far bush and contemplate the universe. When you want me, just call me."

When she spoke again, she was standing on the bank, dressed in Irving's clothes, dampened by her untoweled body and clinging to her boyish figure. Her newly washed hair reached only to her earlobes, like . . . like a stableboy's. So small was she, and how . . . how vulnerable! he thought.

Something in his stare disturbed her. How good he was to her, she thought. But her distress could not have been caused simply by contemplating a good man!

They walked in silence back to the stable, each wrapped in thoughts that could not be shared. By the time they parted at the stable door, the storm clouds were approaching the zenith.

"Quick, inside!" he whispered. "I'll have to run for it." In an attempt to lighten their mood, he added, "Or stay here in the stable all night!"

Neither of them was amused.

16

THE NEXT morning dawned sunny. The clouds had gone, but the mugginess remained in the air, and Lottie knew the stormy weather was not finished with them yet. During what remained of the night before, she had remained wakeful, fearing the lightning, which at times seemed almost to reach in through the tiny window of her refuge.

Stables were always the first to be struck in a storm, she knew, and she kept alert through the night, ready to drop to the floor and leave—first, of course, rescuing the horses.

No such heroic gesture was needed, and she was trudging down the road shortly after daybreak, always heading north, alert for the sounds of wheels behind her. They had fallen into a pattern in only a few days on the road, her rescuer and she, and while she would not presume on his kindness, she was ready to take what was offered.

She had tried to pay him for her meals and lodging at the start, but he would not take the money. But she could refrain from embarrassing him at the various inns, so she would leave early in the morning, maintaining to herself the fiction that she could make it all the way to Pomfret on her own. The curricle had, so far, always caught up with her a mile or two down the road, and she always climbed up to the seat with alacrity.

It was an oddity, she thought, that this pattern

seemed to have taken on the force of habit, as though the pair of them and Irving were destined to ride through life together, always traveling north, always in sunshine.

How fortunate, she thought happily, that her cap had been blown off that second day on the road with him, and her gender if not her identity had been revealed. She was enjoying the company of her rescuer, now that she was no longer confined to the boot.

She did not try to examine her immediate future. She felt oddly light-headed, due of course to the loss of her heavy hair and not in the least to the daring escapade at the river. He had promised to keep his eyes averted, and she believed he had. It was, however, very lowering to perceive that, as a female, she had insufficient attraction to lure him to break his word! She was content for the moment, and she put her feelings out of her mind lest they vanish like soap bubbles.

Before long, she realized that she was foolhardy in the extreme, walking down the road in full view of anyone. She had been frightened the night before by the arrival of Sir Albin. Although this morning she expected to be overtaken by her new friend Sebastian, yet it was more than likely that Sir Albin might well be the next traveler to come along.

Supposing he recognized her, even in Irving's too-large clothes and her short hair? Could she escape him? It was likely that she might, since she knew he was in the vicinity and he could not be sure that she was nearby. Therefore, she was forewarned. But of course the thought that lay at bottom, overlaid by the new contentment that had stolen upon her without her knowing why, must be looked at clearly, in the bright light of day.

She must hide, not only from Sir Albin but also from Sebastian. Sir Albin had caught up with her even though not yet aware of it. And he could well blame Sebastian in some illogical way, perhaps claiming he had kidnapped her. Sir Albin was a violent and extremely dangerous man. She could not bring the wrath of her recent employer down upon her newfound and innocent friend. She was not versed in legal matters, of course, but it was clear that she had no business riding with a gentleman, no matter how kind. He could perhaps be taken up by the authorities for kidnapping her, supposing Sir Albin chose to lay a charge.

She believed that Sir Albin's influence still ran in this district, even though she had not a clear idea of how far they had traveled north, but she did understand that Sir Albin was a dangerous man.

She was enjoying her Gypsy life for the moment, but even while she denied the truth to herself, she had been vaguely aware that this trip was an ephemerally happy time. Sooner or later, she must come down to earth. She suspected that that time had come, sooner than she wished.

Now, of course, she must pick up her independence again, beholden to none for help or companionship. She did so reluctantly. She had spent a long and thoughtful night, full of fears and prey to an active conscience.

She did not walk alone in this life, much as she wanted to. There was her family, to whom she owed more than she could count. And Miss Wythe, whom she had served ill. And, more immediately, she must not burden her new friend with her perilous situation.

She could not believe how much her life had changed. Only a month ago she was watching the seamstress fitting a new ball gown for her sister Carrie, under her mother's watchful eye. There were to be more dresses, cloaks, bonnets—all for the beautiful Carrie.

Lottie had then suppressed the smallest twinge of jealousy. Carrie was the beauty of the family, Carrie would make the best marriage, Carrie must be given her chance. Lottie was already past the first bloom of youth, at least judging by Carrie's fresh loveliness. But as her mother had said, Lottie was too plain ever to be beautiful.

Then Lady Monteagle's machinations had entered her life. Should she have been more biddable, at least given herself the slim chance of eventually receiving Mr. North's offer? She now had firsthand knowledge of the ills of a woman alone in the world. Perhaps her mother was right. Any marriage was better than none. Yet she could not accept such a conclusion.

Since her flight to avoid even meeting the man, she had traveled a path no wellborn young lady would have considered, even had she known such paths existed. Impersonating a governess, even with that lady's encouragement, would shock Lady Forester to her very bones. Now, dressed in stableboy's clothing, riding happily with a gentleman through the countryside, for some days now—entirely unacceptable. She faced her truly desperate situation toward morning, when the storm began to wane.

She had irretrievably lost her reputation. There was nothing she could do to salvage the tiniest shred of respectability.

But even so, she could at least refuse to continue on her scandalous path. Thus it was that she had taken to the road at a very early hour this morning.

She had trudged for some time before she heard the wheels coming behind her. Now she realized that the rig approaching could be either her new friend or Sir Albin himself, clearly on her trail.

Once again, Lottie took to the ditch.

It was as though she were living that first day again. The wheels went past, and then stopped. This time she heard the sound of the curricle backing to stop again, just opposite her hiding place.

The voice—the welcome voice of Sebastian!—called as it had before.

"I've brought you breakfast." Then, in an altered voice, he added quickly, "Get up here, my dear. At once, if you please."

She detected a note of urgency hitherto absent from his voice. She got to her knees and stared up curiously at him. "I don't think so," she told him.

"Don't think. Come on, hurry. Do you want that idiot to find you?"

"How do you know he's after me?"

This curious conversation, he thought, was in a sense more revealing than she knew. There was apparently no question in her mind who *he* was, as he had guessed from her cryptic remark the night before. She had not confided in him, but at least he believed she had something to keep secret. He knew he held a piece of her mysterious past in his hand, and he determined not to let it go.

"Believe me, I know."

She stood up now, longing to take his outstretched hand, and yet listening to her conscience, more active than she thought decent! "There's no need for you to get involved in any troubles," she said firmly.

"It would help, of course, were you to explain to me what your troubles are. But more to the point, why should I not get involved?"

"Because—"

Irving looked back and said, "He's not in sight, sir. Yet."

An odd light danced in Marcus' eyes as he looked down at the slight figure at the edge of the road. He said, "If you do not get in, and *at once*, Irving will lodge a complaint at the next justice of the peace."

"Because I won't ride with you?" she cried, disbelieving.

"For stealing his clothes," said Marcus blandly.

Irving, shocked, cried, "Sir!"

Without a word, measuring the metal of the man

whose hand reached out to hers, she knew when she was beaten. She took his hand and allowed him to pull her up to the seat beside him. She thrust the packet of bread and cheese into her pocket. She might well be hungrier later than she was now.

She turned to Irving, as Marcus set the vehicle in motion, and asked, "Would you indeed charge me with theft?"

"It didn't come to that, now, did it, miss?"

Once again sitting beside Sebastian on the seat, Lottie could allow herself to realize that the man was inordinately attractive to her. Now, if she had been approached, those weeks ago, by this man with an offer to wed, she might well have leapt at the chance. So many times, she thought, one is in the wrong place at the wrong time!

"Have I offended you in some way?" he asked after they had ridden in silence for some time. "Do you regret the loss of your hair?"

He kept his voice low enough so that Irving could not overhear. Marcus began to think that his groom's absence might quite soon prove more welcome than his presence. There were things he might wish to say to his Viola—not now, of course, for there were questions to be answered, and confidence to be won, but . . . in due time.

"No, sir, not in the least. I should have cut it myself, had I had the means." After a pause she added, "You have been more than generous."

"Generous! I hoped you might—" He fell abruptly silent.

These were deep waters he was testing, and he was not sure he wished to probe further, at least just yet. After the intimacy he thought the events of the night before had produced between them, even though he scrupulously had not laid a finger on her, he was disappointed.

pointed. Generous! But he did not know yet what more he wanted of her.

Lottie did not seem to be listening. "I do not even know your name," she said. Then, quickly, lest she be thought forward, she added, "So that I may thank you properly for your kindness."

Marcus, recognizing a diversion when he saw one, followed her lead. "Then I should not know who was thanking me, should I? Since you have not told me your name either."

"Viola," she said in a small voice. "Will that do?"

"Really, my dear," said Marcus, the endearment falling unheeding from his lips, "I cannot believe you were christened that name. It is most unfashionable, you see. A lady is usually named . . ." It was unfortunate that Marcus, not overly imaginative, sought examples in his recent experiences. ". . . Charlotte, or Annabella, or Caroline," he concluded.

"Oh, dear."

Very gently he urged her. "Is it not time to tell me? At the least I should like to know why that very common scoundrel was asking for you at the inn last night?"

Almost, *almost* she did. How good it would be to confide in this very kind man! What a relief she would feel if she could only unburden herself, pick up the load labeled "Sir Albin" and the lesser packet entitled "My Mother" and lay them both on the broad shoulders next to her.

Almost, she did.

But as it happened, her confidences were not destined to be spoken, and in the confusion that ensued, she lost the opportunity of confession.

Irving shouted in alarm, "Stop, sir! Stop!"

She felt the curricle slowing. In a moment the vehicle skewed sideways across the road. Something bumped beneath her, hard, and suddenly Irving was running beside her on the road.

Everything happened at once. Irving holding to the dash in a futile attempt to stop the vehicle, a crashing noise just behind her, the horses neighing and rearing in fright. It seemed a long time ago that she had become aware that the seat was tilting beneath her and the road coming up to meet her.

She reached out blindly to catch hold of something, anything, to break her fall. She felt the rough cloth of Irving's jacket slipping through her fingers, and his face as she saw what he saw—the great wheel, loose from its axle, rolling toward him.

She knew her mouth was open to shout, for she could feel grit on her tongue. But it was Irving who was in peril.

He was in the wrong place. He clutched the spokes as though to stop the wheels by main force, but to no avail. The curricle nearly stopped now, but the horses were still plunging madly, and Marcus' rich voice shouting encouraging words to his cattle had little effect on calming them.

She could only watch, filled with horror, as the wheel inexorably pinned him against the moving vehicle and he went down under the rampaging wheel.

Lottie saw that much, saw the look of excruciating pain on the groom's face, knew that her seat was tilting drastically and she was losing her grip on it.

She felt herself sailing effortlessly through the air. Treetops whirled above her as though she were on a roundabout. She landed with a jolt that shook the breath from her, and then the darkness came.

Lottie woke to leafy skies overhead, and a far-off murmur of voices. Angry voices. Voices recognizable, but very angry.

She would simply lie here for a moment until she knew where she was. Sailing through the air—she remembered that. And something about a wheel . . .

It all came back with a jolt.

The wheel had come off the curricle, and the horses, frightened out of what little wits horses possess, had bolted. Only that firm hand on the reins had kept them all from disaster.

Where was he? Was he hurt? Certainly Irving had been badly injured—she had seen his face as he went down.

The voices grew louder now. She raised herself on an elbow, the better to hear. How her head ached! She must have hit a rock, or at the least a tree root, when she fell. Fortunately, the mass of remaining hair piled up under the cap she wore had saved her from more severe damage. But there was no time to contemplate her injuries, for the speakers on the road were becoming heated.

Sir Albin's voice: "Too bad, such a tragic accident. Is he dead? I should not have thought you could manage your cattle so well."

"One needs to, apparently," said the voice of her friend. "If there is villainy abroad."

Sir Albin maintained his good humor. Lottie could almost see that vulpine grin of his. She trembled for Sebastian.

One thing she was sure of. Sir Albin did not know she was nearby. Her rescuer had apparently dragged her farther into the woods from the place she had landed, to keep her out of the view of Sir Albin, who he knew was following. Certainly he and Irving had been expecting him.

Poor Irving! She ought to hurry to him to attend him until a doctor could be summoned—but then she realized that she could return Sebastian's kindness with an equal generosity of her own.

All her overnight doubts, all her reluctance to continue on the path she had been traveling, and yet her equal unwillingness to abandon her new companion, came to a head. She knew, indeed had known for some time, what she must do, and she knew that now was the time.

Taking great care to avoid the slightest rustling underfoot, so as not to give away her presence or her intentions to the men on the road, she stole away in a direction opposite to the road, trusting to the argument now fading behind her, and to the required care for Irving, to keep the men busy until she was safely away.

Soon she reached the far edge of the woods. A rolling field stretched before her, and she could see no houses, no buildings, not even a stray animal.

Well, this uncharted field, so to speak, was like her own plans—without features and without direction.

She was running away again, and this time she was running away from Sir Albin's threats, as well as her mother's disapproval, but she knew that she was also running away from herself, her mixed-up feelings about Sebastian, and from Sebastian himself. She could not sort it all out, but she knew the first thing to do was to get well away from the two men left behind.

Taking a deep breath, she strode, with a confidence she felt not at all, onto the field.

17

SHE WALKED all day.

Surprisingly, she still had Marcus' bread and cheese in her pocket. The fall had flattened the bread, but it was all there, and she attacked it ravenously in a hedge when the sun was high overhead.

She was becoming adept as a Gypsy, she thought with a touch of satisfaction, at moving safely through the countryside. Now, if she only knew where she was!

Pomfret lay ahead, she was sure. When she reached the vicinity of Castleton, she would turn left . . . or make discreet inquiry . . . or decide what to do when she got there.

At the moment, Pomfret filled her mind, like the towers of a fantasy city not seen, but known to be somewhere in the mists of the future, a city where all troubles would be ended and peace would abound.

The only trouble was that she was not certain she wished to settle for peace. The end of all troubles was tempting. of course, but did she really want that? She remembered reading somewhere that if one did not suffer, then how did he know he was alive?

She knew, all right. At least these last few days had taught her that life contained happiness, contentment, optimism, and perhaps another quality or two that she did not know how to put a name to. But while Pomfret might not be all she hoped, yet it was all she had of any certainty at the moment. When she arrived at what was, after all, her own property, to which she could resort or leave, precisely as she chose, she would know better what to do.

The first thing to do would be to rest. She was far more tired than she had thought. Surely a healthy young lady might walk or ride all day long without collapsing from fatigue?

But it was the emotional strain, first from her mother, then from Sir Albin, and latterly, but in a different way, from her good friend Sebastian, that wreaked havoc. She knew she had a mere shred of reputation left— unless by some evil chance her jaunt through the country lanes with Sebastian came to light.

In that case, she would in all likelihood have to immure herself like a medieval nun. Perhaps, if she were to refuse to explain her recent whereabouts, no one would know that she had traveled across a quarter of the country in the unhallowed company of a gentleman whose name she did not know.

All to the good, however—she reflected—he did not know her name either.

Night was near, and still she had not come to any town. She wondered whether she was walking in a circle, as lost persons were said to do, but she remembered that always she had had the sun in the correct place in the sky. It would be better to travel by night, for the stars could serve as an infallible guide, but she could not bring herself to venture out on the dark roads. She was not as brave as she pretended.

She must soon find shelter for the night. Not another haymow! She was so *weary* of the fresh scent of hay warmed by the sun, the barn dust in her nostrils!

She estimated that since she had been going northwest, away from the road she had been on, she might well be nearing Pomfret. She wished she had a better knowledge of her country. It was all very well to point out an orange shape on a globe and say with assurance, "There lies Arabia Felix." It was quite another to say, "Castleton lies twenty (or thirty) leagues from here, and Pomfret would be just *there*."

She crested a small rise that marked the end of the most recent field she had crossed, taking care not to trample the growing crops. Below her abruptly opened a lane, not even wide enough for a cart. She eyed it dubiously. Would it be safe to leave her fields?

But the lane must run somewhere, and perhaps she could inquire about Castleton—how far was it, how long would it take to arrive? She might even, so far away from the road they had traveled, take a room in an unpretentious inn. She still had the money she had had in her pocket when she left Drysdale House. She could afford a decent room.

While she stood contemplating the lane, she did not see the approach of a man. He was, when she took note of him, a sturdy figure, thick legs and arms like those of a blacksmith, or of a hard worker, in any event.

His eyes gave her pause. They were bright, curious, and in a way predatory. She was reminded of a raven eyeing a succulent grasshopper.

She turned and ran. She could hear him clambering up the steep bank from the lane and pounding after her. The chase was short, and its conclusion foregone.

Holding her ear painfully between thick thumb and forefinger, he held her as though with a tether. "Now then, m'boy, who be ye?"

Resigned, at least for the moment, to her fate, she borrowed another name. "Tyson," she muttered. "John Tyson." Echoing her captor, she demanded of him, "And who be *ye*?"

"Parish officer. Name of Rockwell."

Under her breath she said, "Good God! Could anything be worse?" Aloud she said, "I'm going to Castleton. Which way shall I go, right or left?"

"Castleton? Hah! You be going to the workhouse."

"W-workhouse?" Her voice was a mere whisper.

"Vagrant, you see. They'll be glad enough of an extra hand there, I've no doubt."

At last she had come to the end of her rope. She could go no further. No kindly gentleman was likely to arise out of the ground and beguile her with Shakespearean nicknames and pleasant converse. It was useless to advance her Forester claim, since she was not anxious to be laughed at.

The man regarded her with misgivings. There would be brutal treatment for one as slight as this one in the workhouse. Surely the lad had done nothing criminal. A plan to his own advantage budded in his mind.

"You could come as kitchen boy to the George and Dragon," he offered.

"Kitchen boy? I don't think so . . . that is, I don't think I'd be any good at it."

"One way to find out—learn how."

She was sorry she had spoken at the beginning. If she had remained silent, and never vouchsafed a word, no one could inform Lady Forester that her eldest daughter had been found inexplicably alone and in borrowed clothes, probably the victim of unspeakable vileness. No one would spoil Carrie's chances of marriage. "Only a fool would offer for that one," people would say. "Her sister's been *put away*." In the workhouse! Or toiling in a kitchen!

"Hey!" said her captor. "Cat got your tongue? Well, no matter to me. I'm that tired of hearing complaints. But I wager you'll be no better than the rest of 'em, young man, when you get into the workhouse."

Then, relenting, he urged, "But maybe the workhouse is too hard for you. Best try kitchen boy. Here, take off your cap so's I can see what you look like."

Not a likely-looking boy at first glance, but some of

them wiry ones were foolers. Lottie's cap was removed, and a ragged mane of hair fell almost to the thin shoulders.

"That's the strangest head I ever seen!" Then the truth dawned. "Good God, it's a girl!"

Later, when he had marched her, not by the ear but with a heavy hand on her thin shoulder, to his own hostelry, called the George and Dragon, he put his hands on his hips and looked down at her.

"Well, then, what do you say? Can you bide working here?"

She found her voice. "As a kitchen boy? I warn you, I am not used to such work, and I may not do well. Could you not let me go on to Castleton? You would not then be troubled with me."

His eyebrows lifted. "I thought I heard a gentle tongue then, up on the hill. I wonder whose family is wondering where their daughter is tonight."

"I am an orphan," she said bravely.

Her chin quivered, and he laughed. "Don't get in a fever about it. It's worth my life to monkey around with a young female." He cast his eyes towards the ceiling. "My lady friend, you know. Can't have her dropping in on me unexpected and finding a morsel like you playing cozy. If you catch my meaning."

"I don't suppose you will simply let me go?"

"Not a chance. I'll be bound you're willing enough, when you see your choice clear."

"The workhouse?"

"Or the kitchen."

He leaned back in his chair. He knew which she would choose, and there was no harm in watching her mental struggle. Just so a cat toys with a mouse, knowing the ultimate outcome.

Lottie regarded her employment, such as it was, as temporary. She would stay not a day more than it suited her. Her plan was simple, as it had to be. She would arm herself with a kitchen knife, and when the occasion demanded, defend herself with it. She was no longer confident that her boyish disguise was sufficient. It had been penetrated at least twice.

She was thwarted in the second part of her plan, however, to take to the road upon the first occasion presenting itself. Rockwell would not allow her to sleep in the stable. "Aha, I see your game!" he said genially. "You'll sleep in the attic, where I can lock you in at night."

"Why?"

"Good help, and cheap at that, is hard to find. And don't think to slough off the work either, or you'll have a clout on the ear faster than you can see it coming."

For the next few days, Lottie, still in Irving's clothes, newly washed, scoured tables, mopped floors, served food and drink, and climbed the stairs to her attic room at night, ready to drop. Even had she been sleeping in the stable, she would have lacked strength enough to walk out of the yard.

There was one party she was never allowed to serve. The squire came in a few times, and Rockwell banished her to the kitchen on each occasion.

"Stay there," he admonished her, raising his hamlike hand as though to cuff her. "I'll wait on Squire myself."

Muttering to himself, he said, "How did I get into such a coil? If she's a boy, then squire with his funny ways won't take no for an answer. If she's a girl—which she doubtless is—and *they* find out about it, I'll be up afore Magistrate on scandal charges and lose my parish job to boot."

He wished he had never fallen into this mess, but the boy—that is, the girl—was the best help he had ever had. He had not the slightest doubt that she was gently bred, and it was surprising that she could work so well. Besides, he consoled himself, somewhere there would be a family ready to ransom her, if he could just find out who they were.

18

A T THIS moment, Lottie considered herself safe. Dressed in boy's clothes, working hard at the George and Dragon, she believed that Sir Albin Drysdale would never find her.

He had come all too close the day the wheel had fallen off Sebastian's curricle. If her new friend had not had the presence of mind to carry her half-conscious body out of the roadway, she would have been discovered. And then what would have happened, she did not wish to contemplate.

Sir Albin figured in her thoughts, however, less than did Sebastian. That foolish fiction! She as Viola and he as Sebatian did very well while they were traveling together the length of England, but certainly she wished now she knew his true name. It was only deep within her that she began to wonder whether he really played, unwittingly of course, the role of Duke Orsino.

Another day or two on the road, she suspected, and their arm's-length relationship might well have broken down, at least on her part, into something more vital. Inexperienced as she was, she recalled with some uneasiness that moonlit night on the stream bank where she had lost her hair, her grime, and her serenity. Very conscious that night of Sebastian's clean scent, the disturbing expression in his eyes as he looked at her in her clingingly damp clothes—the moon had been *very* bright—she could not shake the bewildering sense that she had somehow crossed into a new existence.

And, she told herself, suppose he turned out to be ineligible? Married, for instance?

For of all things he longed for, he had told her, was his own fireside, his own family around him. Suppose he already had his heart's desire?

Lottie grabbed the broom and wielded it fiercely across the kitchen floor. Sebastian was a part of her past, admittedly a very pleasant part, and she would simply have to stay here in safety and in anonymity until she was assured that Sir Albin had given up his pursuit of "Miss Wythe."

While Lottie worked hard for her daily bread—what there was of it—and was locked into the attic room every night, lonely and certain that she had been forgotten by everyone, much activity was taking place at a distance, a good deal of it concerning her.

A primary, and urgent, matter of these various activities was being pressed by Marcus North.

Marcus, having seen to the most urgent of his responsibilities and summoned a physician to the side of his injured groom, expected to see Lottie hovering somewhere around the perimeter of the innyard. Irving was, happily, not seriously injured, even though the accident could have been deadly. The doctor, pronouncing that the broken leg could not be moved without permanent damage, was pleased to accept a handsome retainer in return for a promise to take the greatest care of his patient.

Making arrangements also with the innkeeper for his servant's care, Marcus was at last free to search for Lottie.

He had pulled her away from the roadside just in time, for he heard the wheels of Sir Albin's vehicle approaching. He rightly had a strong suspicion as to the cause of her wheel's coming loose, for Irving took care with the vehicles under his supervision, and a loose wheel was not to be expected.

Sir Albin, balked of his sitting room the night before, was capable, in Marcus' judgment, of taking a dastardly revenge, wreaking punishment indiscriminately even on persons who had never injured him.

But it was instinct with Marcus to remove his Viola from the scene. If Sir Albin caught sight of her, the fat would be in the fire indeed. While Marcus did not know the details of the encounter that had spawned this vicious pursuit, and Viola's clear fear of a pursuer was so far unidentified, it did not occur to him to seek enlightenment from Sir Albin. If Viola did not wish to confide in him, then he would not pry.

Some hours had passed since the wheel had fallen off the curricle, and it was repaired now and ready to take the road. Marcus held a strong wish for revenge on the dastard, but there would be time enough later to hunt him down and call him to account. The man had come upon the scene of the accident soon after it happened and directly after Marcus had removed Viola from the scene. Fortunately a farm cart had come along in time to take Irving back to the inn, so that Marcus was not in debt to Sir Albin for his assistance.

There would be a time for Sir Albin. First, Marcus must find the girl. He expected her to rise from the ditch at his approach or—supposing she was not sure of the approaching vehicle—to lie hidden until he came for her. She could surely have no doubt that he would come for her as soon as he was able.

However, the miles unrolled before him, and vanished behind him, slowly, for he was scanning the sides of the road to catch the first sight of his passenger.

At length, when some distance had been covered, he realized that his Viola had not waited along the road for him. His disappointment was like an unexpected knife in his chest.

How could she not have trusted him? Very easily, he realized.

The road turned away to the east, and he traveled on with diminishing hope.

For a man unused to introspection, he realized, he had probed himself deeply enough not to be pleased with what he discovered. He had not expected to understand women. Women were, as he had always been taught, fickle, bubble-headed, subject to hysterical fits, and resistant to all education and common sense. Logic and women were like two words in separate languages —no connection whatever.

However, his recent passenger had belied such belief, and he began to think he had much to learn about the female gender. She had introduced him to lively conversation, sharing her well-informed mind with him, and treated him like an equal. To his surprise, he regarded the latter as a compliment.

In short, the young lady, whoever she might be, was no ordinary female. And he missed her sorely.

Although he was not yet ready to admit it, Marcus was undergoing a thorough reorganization, even renovation. He had all but forgotten the empty-headed Annabella; and even his thoughts about the young lady who had refused even to meet him, considering him not worth the while, were mellowing. He could not be as arrogant as the man in the inn, but in his own way—he began to see—he had been selfish and inconsiderate.

He did not know what he would do when he found the girl again. He did not entertain for more than a moment the thought that he might not find her, ever. First things first, he decided, and his primary need was to find her and protect her from the myriad of pitfalls that lay in wait for a trusting young lady.

He knew she was wellborn. She could not disguise her voice, her manner, under those disreputable boy's clothes. But she had never trusted him sufficiently to tell him her name.

How could he find her? She had not traveled along the road. Unless she had been picked up by another man in a curricle. His thoughts focused ominously on the villain who had caused the accident. Now he began to realize that perhaps the villain had more on his mind than simple juvenile revenge.

Suppose he had planned the incident so he could get hold of Marcus' young lady?

The phrase echoed in his mind, not distastefully— "my young lady." It had a nice ring to it!

Marcus drove all the way to Castleton before he cast his net wider. He was inexperienced in the ways of detection, but he had met the girl in connection with an inn, and it seemed logical to search in the same *milieu* to find her again.

At Castleton he made inquiries, and, turning back on the way he had come, he made more futile inquiries. One inn after another was crossed off his mental list. He inquired at three White Harts, one Little White Hart, and two Seven Stars. His Viola was not to be found at the Goose and Gridiron, nor at the Flying Horse. Nor were his inquiries successful at more Saracen's Heads than could have been found in Turkey.

But, having made futile inquiries for the better part of four days, he had at last, with the utmost reluctance, given up the idea of tracing his Viola.

He set his face toward Gresham Manor, planning to send someone back for his injured groom, and to try, if he could, to forget the events of this journey.

He was still half a day from home, and he was too dispirited to drive on into the night in the dark of the moon and over roads miry from recent rains. It was not as if there would be love and a warm welcome waiting for him. Instead, he thought, glancing at the sky, he would as likely as not be drenched by the storm that was coming up.

Shelter, in the form of the George and Dragon, loomed just ahead of him.

In another part of England, Lottie's safety was a matter of deep concern. Lady Forester was seriously alarmed by the disappearance of her eldest daughter. Her urgent letter to Lady Drysdale had elicited no response, not even a civil acknowledgement of its arrival.

"That's what comes of having no man in the family," she told the portrait of her husband. "If you hadn't died, Lottie would never have dared to run away, and she wouldn't be lost now, in God knows what kind of dreadful circumstances. And I wouldn't have to try to find her!" This scolding was the nearest thing to regret over her husband's death that she had admitted for ten years.

Tyson wished to accompany her on her planned journey. He expected little from the arrival of Lady Forester at the place where Miss Lottie had been—as a governess, if one could believe Miss Wythe. Tyson's original idea, of traveling himself with an armed escort to exact, preferably by force, information needed to find the young miss, had been vetoed by his mistress.

"You must stay here, Tyson, and manage things. Who knows, Miss Lottie may find her way back here. I want you to be here to see to . . . what might be needed." Unspoken between them lay the dread possibilities of Miss Lottie wounded, ill, or even worse.

"Very good, my lady," Tyson agreed without enthusiasm.

So it was that about the time Sir Albin was viewing the curricle accident on the road, the result of his surreptitious loosening of the wheel, Lady Forester was setting out from Pentstable to retrieve her daughter from whatever pit of evil she might have fallen into.

Her first stop of course was Miss Wythe's cottage in Alford. Miss Wythe was not overjoyed to see her.

"I suppose you believe the fault is to be laid at my door," said Miss Wythe, on the principle of the best defense being a spirited attack. "Well, I suppose it is, but had the child not been miserable . . ."

Lady Forester's eyes narrowed to slits, and one toe tapped on the floor. But since she was not for the most part a foolish woman, she bit the words back.

"It does no good, Miss Wythe, to exchange recriminations. I confess we are both vulnerable to blame, but that will not get our girl back. Now, why not fix us both a dish of tea, and you may tell me precisely what happened."

Miss Wythe was not anxious for a *tête-à-tête* with Lottie's mother. "But your horses, Lady Forester? Should they be allowed to stand?"

"We will let Coachman worry about that. I expect the tale is soon told, and I will be on my way."

The tea was hot and restorative, and as predicted, Miss Wythe's tale, shorn of any speculation on the reasons for Lottie's flight from Pentstable, was soon told.

"So," said Lady Forester thoughtfully, "you have no idea why Lottie left the Drysdales? That woman, no doubt. She didn't even acknowledge my letter!"

"The entire business is a mystery to me," agreed Miss Wythe. "But she was obviously paid for her time there." She explained the hoard of money found in the trunk. "And a little extra, which may have been a sop for an abrupt dismissal."

"I wonder—since Lottie did not return to you, and she did not come back to Pentstable, then—where could she go?"

"She did say," volunteered the governess, "when she first came, that she had considered the Priory."

"Pomfret?"

"She said it was her own property. But it did not seem to me that she was serious about traveling so far, and to such a reclusive spot, too."

"Perhaps she thought so then," said Lady Forester acutely, "but clearly her situation has been altered, by her own plan or by necessity."

"You think she may have gone north?" Miss Wythe asked with dawning hope. Pomfret might be out of the way, but certainly if Lottie had arrived there, she was not confined to a sordid tenement, or captive of a highwayman, or . . . Miss Wythe's imagination did not provide any more desperate pictures than those. However, she did believe that if Lottie had arrived at Pomfret she would have sent word to her mother, and to herself.

"I shall depart at once for Pomfret," Lady Forester said with determination. "I cannot think I will learn anything from that Drysdale woman, and I shall not trouble her unless I arrive at Pomfret and find no word of Lottie."

Both women considered for a moment the precarious situation of a well-brought-up young lady, alone, wearing a gray muslin gown, and parted from her trunk with all her possessions in it.

Lady Forester said, with wry humor, "She'll be glad of a change of clothes by now, I suspect!"

Lottie's mother, steadfastly refusing to consider the various fates that might have befallen her daughter, traveled north on the road that would lead eventually to Pomfret. Castleton was her immediate goal. She remembered that one turned left in the town, and from there half a day's journey would bring her to Pomfret.

It had been a long time since she had traveled north to her mother-in-law's girlhood home, but she had a tongue in her head, and directions could be inquired for.

The late spring had turned into a rainy summer. Storms moved at times across the face of England, and she could only hope that for a sennight the skies might remain unclouded.

For three days she was fortunate. The coach made good time, and they were at last approaching Castleton. She had made inquiries about Lottie—more tactfully than had Sir Albin—along the way.

No one had set eyes on a solitary woman traveling by stage, or, more ominously, in company in a private vehicle. Lottie seemed to have disappeared as though she had never existed.

But Lady Forester, conscious of an emptiness in her heart where Lottie had been, set her mind stolidly on the expectation that the girl was already at Pomfret.

She felt the coach slowing now, and finally it stopped. Letting down the curtains, she waited for Coachman to approach.

"They's been rain lately, my lady," said he, "and the road's getting muddier all the time. Cattle are tired enough already."

"What do you want to do? I cannot dry the roads for you."

"No, my lady. But it comes to me to stop for the night afore we get into Castleton."

"Where, though? I suspect this country is fairly lacking in decent hostelries."

"Yonder is one, looks respectable, my lady."

She glanced down the road ahead at the building he indicated. At least the grounds seemed to show some tending, and she knew that Coachman would not suggest stopping unless the horses truly needed the rest.

She nodded permission, and in a few moments Lady Forester's coach turned unsuspectingly into the stable-yard of the George and Dragon.

* * *

Surprisingly, Albin Drysdale's path as he pursued his own investigation did not cross that of Marcus North. While he made inquiry of the same inns, somewhat to the irritation of landlords faced with two inquiries from different gentlemen about, of all things, a stableboy on the one hand, and a lady in flight on the other, he was never at the same inn as Marcus at the same time.

While an ordinary man might well have given up days ago, feeling the game was not worth the candle, Albin was no ordinary man. The one woman who had scorned him, who had lied to him in telling him she was a mere governess, thus concealing her real situation in life from him, must be brought to admit her transgressions.

His scheme, scarcely altered from the start, had one goal: the humbling of the pretended governess. It would be an added benefit, he thought, could he marry her first, get Pomfret Priory into his own hands, and then deal with her as she deserved.

But to accomplish this goal, he must find her.

His continued good fortune in not meeting the man whose wheel he had loosened could not continue. But, unaware that Marcus was in pursuit of the same lady as his own prey, he felt he was safe from pursuit and could take up his inquiries about Miss Forester.

He had no idea that Miss Forester had transformed herself, to all appearances, into a stableboy. He did have, however, a shrewd idea of her destination. He had known other women—granted, they were not gentlewomen for the most part, but women were women, after all—and when women were injured, or despised, or troubled, they were as one in seeking shelter and comfort, rather like a vixen seeking her den.

Since Miss Forester had not returned to Alford, nor to her home, she was undoubtedly hastening to Pomfret. Albin was pleased with his acumen. He would of course continue his search for her on the road to

Pomfret, hoping to reach her before she reached shelter. But in the long run he was sure he would have her. He could, in the end, simply go to Pomfret himself and wait for her. Once he had her in her own house, unprotected save by servants, he could force her to marry him.

And then, as soon as the vows were spoken, she would feel his wrath, the stronger for having been postponed for so long, and afterward, if she survived his treatment, he would leave her there while he made free with her property.

A smile twisted his full lips. He really did not care whether she survived or not. He would have his revenge on her, and Pomfret Priory as a bonus.

It was chance that brought Albin Drysdale to the George and Dragon. He had exhausted his possibilities on the road north to Castleton, and since he knew her destination, he had taken a detour onto a road she might have found more direct.

He was making his way gradually, forcing himself to be thorough, toward Pomfret. He could afford to take his time, since he was sure of his prey in the end.

The George and Dragon was not more ramshackle than others of its kind, being off the main road and in all likelihood serving as a resort for the local inhabitants.

Albin drove in, looking around him with a slight curl to his lips. He paused in the yard, waiting for a stableboy to come to take the reins.

Fortunately for Lottie, glancing out into the yard with some apprehension as she did whenever she heard wheels crunching in the dirt, the stableboy was laggard, and she had time to recognize the newcomer.

Good God! It was Albin Drysdale!

She was desperate. She must fly at once! But where? Sir Albin was already crossing the yard. Lottie grabbed Rockwell's key and fled to her attic room, locking the door from the inside. She believed the landlord would not betray her presence to any stranger, since she had no illusions as to her value to him as an unpaid servant. She suspected, in addition, that his position as parish officer for the poor might be in jeopardy, were his use of her to his advantage discovered by the authorities.

But she had no such trust in Sir Albin. He was fully capable, if he knew she was there, of coming up the stairs and breaking down her door. She had, of course, no idea that he had Pomfret in his sights as a target, since she believed him unaware of her identity. But revenge for her turning him down, as well as slashing him across the face with what was at bottom his own whip, provided the strongest of motivations for him

She stole across her attic, avoiding the boards that squeaked, and knelt on the floor next to the small window that looked out on the yard below. She took care not to be seen, but she needed to know when Sir Albin left. Until that time, she was a prisoner, by her own choice, in her attic.

Below her, Rockwell had come into the yard to greet the new arrival. To his dismay, the newcomer began at once, in a boorish accusing way, to demand news of a certain young woman who had probably taken rooms at this inn—so Albin said—recently.

"No, sir, I know of no woman like that."

"Are you really as stupid as you look?" asked Albin at last sneering in frustration. "Nobody can be that doltish! You give me reason to suspect—just by playing dumb, you fool!—that you are fully aware of the woman I'm looking for. Not above average height, skinny as a boy, white streak in her hair . . ."

The landlord's face, previously wearing an expression of obsequious attention, now went blank. This man was after his John Tyson, and although Rockwell would never admit it, he had taken a fancy to the lass. Not in *that* way, he amended, but he was sure he was not going to give the lass away to this man, whose looks he did not in the least like. This man was jumped-up quality, not real, and indeed was likely no better than the squire, who was, in Rockwell's mind, a right villain.

"What would such a woman be doing here?" he said reasonably. "We don't see many of the gentry passing by. Once last year we had a party—"

"Your party be damned. Where's the wench?"

"I tell you—"

"Don't tell me anything, you idiot! Just fetch her!"

Albin had no real suspicion that Lottie was here. He was simply proceeding in his usual style, in the only way he knew to extract information from an unwilling subject.

"She's not here!"

Albin abandoned verbal inquiry. He grabbed the landlord's vest with one hand, and made the other hand into a fist and shook it under the bulbous nose.

"Got a pigsty?" demanded Sir Albin crudely. "That's where I ought to throw you!"

Instead, he tightened his grip on Rockwell's vest and shook him, then shoved him roughly so that he fell sprawling onto the ground.

This was the tableau that greeted Marcus as he drove through the innyard gate.

19

LOTTIE, PEERING furtively from her attic window onto the scene below, was at once terrified and fascinated. Below her, her nemesis stood triumphantly over the landlord, supine on the ground. At the gate to the yard a guest was arriving, driving a curricle and a splendid pair.

And she could also see, on the road beyond, a coach and four slowing for the inn. She would be needed in the kitchen, but how could she leave the haven of her attic?

Her eyes focused on the curricle and pair just coming in, the horses picking their way delicately through the mud of the yard. Surely she recognized that rig!

She leaned from her window, the better to see. Good God! It was Sebastian!

She withdrew into the room, but too late. Marcus' attention had been caught by the quick movement at the window. She was utterly bewildered. How was it that Sir Albin had traced her here, but more than that, how could Sebastian have found her? Her education included work on the globe, and she could point with sure finger to the site of Calcutta, or Shanghai, or Melbourne. But she did not know that by great good fortune she had come to an inn on the direct road to Pomfret Priory.

The landlord, lying on the ground, was yet finely tuned to the advent of custom. He cried out in sheer frustration when he saw, approaching behind his tormentor, not only Marcus' elegant vehicle but also just now a splendid coach and four coming through the gate! Surely fortune had chosen an inappropriate time to shower him with a surplus of prosperous guests!

Marcus, taking in the situation before him, acted automatically. Part of his mind was telling him that he had found his Viola, upstairs, of all inexplicable places, in this very inn. That movement at the window had been brief—but he would know his lady anywhere, no matter how dimly seen!

Just now, there was the simple chore of disposing of this arrogant bully. Marcus grabbed Sir Albin by the shoulder and turned him to face him.

Sir Albin, beside himself with frustrated fury, did not wait to see his attacker. He brought up a fist even as he turned, and buried it in Marcus' midriff.

The landlord, seeing his attacker otherwise occupied, scrambled to his feet and ran to open the coach door for the aristocratic party.

The lady's voice rose plaintively from within. "Are you sure this is a respectable place?"

Rockwell, bowing at the door, assured her he ran an honest establishment. "That," he said, waving a hand at the combatants, "is just a little disagreement among gentlemen."

"Gentlemen indeed!" said Lady Forester. She looked more closely at them. The victor, standing triumpantly over his fallen foe, she did not know. But the man on the ground . . . She gasped in disbelief. Surely she must be mistaken! But on second look, she knew she was right. Marcus North, Lady Monteagle's precious protégé, was flat on his back in the muddy stableyard.

She breathed a sigh of relief. At least Lottie was not betrothed to the man!

Marcus was oblivious of the coach and four behind him. He had seen Viola upstairs, he was sure of it. And to leave her unprotected with this great blot on the earth to do what he would with her . . . It was not to be thought of!

Fueled by his joy at finding Viola again, his fear for what this idiot might do to her, and a simple masculine desire for revenge against the man who had made him look so ineffectual, Marcus scrambled to his feet in one smooth movement, the end of which resulted in a satisfactory crunch of his fist into Sir Albin's taunting smile.

Stepping over the prostrate body of his foe, Marcus hurried into the inn, to race up the stairs to find his girl.

But Lottie, overjoyed at seeing him again, and fearless now that Sir Albin had been bested, met Marcus at the foot of the stairs. She flew into his arms, and he folded her close to him.

"How did you find me?" she asked at last, and then realized that she was taking his arrival too much for granted. "But perhaps," she amended shyly, "you were not looking for me?"

"Indeed I was," he told her firmly. "After I got Irving settled, and found you gone . . ." He stopped short. He had no intention of telling her that he had approached lunacy too nearly for his peace of mind. His girl had vanished, and he had been frantic—but now he thought perhaps he had taken too much for granted. *Was* she his girl?

He looked down into her face. "You're thinner," he said tenderly. "I cannot think what you are doing here, but you will tell me some day."

Some day! The lovely thought conjured up an entire future in one beatific vision—time enough to explore the past, marvel over the miracles that had brought them together, and dream of their joined future. *Some day!* Surely he intended for them to be together?

"Some day," she agreed happily.

Lottie's doubts, her unhappiness, even Albin Drysdale, as well as the source of her flight from Pentstable,

Marcus North—all drained away as Sebastian continued to hold her in his arms.

She had thought she could never be happy again. She had never expected to fall in love, if that was the term to describe her feelings. But certainly she was a different person from the girl who had thought all her problems would be solved if she could only run away from them. Running away had brought her to hardships, poverty, drudgery, but also it had brought her Sebastian for a few days. And now, here he was again, coming for her as though he were a knight in shining armor, instead of a kind and considerate gentleman in an unobtrusively smart curricle pulled by a pair of grays instead of the traditional white horse. But the emendations did not count. The basic truth was unaltered.

Miracles could happen!

From far away came the unmistakable sounds connected with the new arrivals. Coach doors slammed, voices, Rockwell escorting the lady into the inn, extolling its virtues.

"This is no place for us," said Marcus. "I have no wish to meet anyone. Particularly that idiot who seems to think with his fists."

"What *do* you wish, Sebastian?"

"Sebastian?" He quirked an eyebrow. "We shall have to discuss Sebastian."

"Oh, yes!" she breathed.

"But not here."

He drew her with him down the hall toward the back door. Feeling her slight body warm against his own, and knowing at last that he could protect her against her pursuer, he stopped short. He cupped her face in his hands, and, seeing an encouraging light in her eyes, gently kissed her. At the start it was intended to be a brief touching of lips, but it soon turned into a much more substantial embrace. Her arms stole upward to encircle his neck, and he pressed her close to him.

Only Marcus heard the indrawn gasp from the direction of the entrance door, and he glanced over Lottie's head, fearing for the moment to see Sir Albin, recovered and thirsting for vengeance.

The face that was turned his way was not that of Sir Albin. He gazed with disbelief, followed by appalled recognition.

Good God! he thought. It's Lady Forester!

Disaster, thought Marcus, seconds later, had its humorous side. But there would be time to laugh hereafter, supposing of course that he and Lottie were able to escape.

Whirling Lottie around so that his body shielded her, he thrust her out the door into the darkening yard beyond. He hoped devoutly that Lady Forester had not recognized Lottie. He had no such hope regarding himself. He had seen a flare of recognition in Lady Forester's eyes, standing as she was in the full light of the lamps, that told him she had indeed recognized Marcus North, a man she had considered as a possible suitor for her daughter Lottie. And there was no hope that she had not seen him passionately embracing—and that kiss, a revelation to him, had undoubtedly been, on both sides, exceptionally enthusiastic—a person who appeared to be, at least from a distance, a kitchen boy.

Outside the inn, Marcus was stirred deeply by the trusting expression of his Viola. "Why are we rushing so?" she asked him. Could it have been that he wished more privacy for them? The thought was delicious, and she shivered in anticipation.

But if he wished privacy, it was not for tender purposes. Instead, he grabbed her hand and urged her to a run. Around the stable they went, through what seemed to her like a kitchen midden, skirting a noisome pond, and on to a lane cut deeply into the earth by centuries of plodding feet.

At length, out of breath, she gasped, "Can't we stop? I can't run anymore!"

At once he slowed to a walk. "I'm sorry, but we had to leave in a hurry."

"I noticed," she said dryly. "Was it Sir Albin? He would not have dared fight again."

"No," agreed Marcus. "Is that his name? I suspect he is a bully, lording it over those who are in his power."

"As I was," she said incautiously. She had not revealed the reasons for his determined chase.

Marcus reflected. Apparently she had not been aware of the lady who had come into the inn, nor of the remark that came only too clearly to Marcus' ears. He had pushed the girl out-of-doors before those autocratic tones came to her ears. "I thought this was a respectable inn. But *manifestly* I was wrong!"

He needed to think. He required a vehicle, preferably his own excellent one at the George and Dragon. And he needed to be sure this girl, whose name was certainly not Viola, would be safe and not run away again while he was gone.

He exacted her promise before he left her in the dark shadow cast by a small tree leaning over the lane. It would be full night before he could extricate his horse from the stable and his curricle from the yard, and the darkness would, he hoped, conceal him from the lady he had so inadvertently shocked.

Marcus lingered outside the stable in the shadows while he gave himself over to concentrated thought.

He recalled remarks made by Viola as they had traveled north. Ladies married off as in a cattle market, she had commented; young, inexperienced misses wed for their property. And the prime statement that should have set off bells in his head as though ringing loudly in a cathedral: ladies offered for in order to round out an estate!

Viola had said these things, but he would bet his life that it was Charlotte Forester who had jaunted with him in the most scandalous fashion possible. But perhaps not as scandalous as the interpretation Lady Forester might put upon the scene she had witnessed! He grinned at the recollection.

That anyone could think him capable of that particular depravity!

But it was not that last scene that troubled him deeply. He had always considered himself a staid supporter of law and order, of society the way it was, even a victim of convention! And now here he was, a prosaic and unheroic gentleman, in a fix he could never have dreamed of!

But he knew one thing. They were very near to their destination—Pomfret a mere half-day's travel away, even less by shortcuts he knew, and Gresham just beyond the Priory. He could easily escort her to her estate. But what would happen after that?

He had no illusions. Miss Forester—his Viola!—had clearly ruined her reputation by haring around the countryside, the two of them together, as though they were Adam and Eve, although more suitably dressed, and no one else existed in the world. They had been happy days, the happiest he had ever experienced. Even though they had been Sebastian and Viola, keeping to those roles of brother and sister, he now knew that the Duke Orsino was his proper position. He was in love, desperately and for all time, with this slip of a girl, whom—the thought came to him suddenly—he had never seen in a dress!

He was convinced now that his Viola was Charlotte Forester—both by what she had said and equally what she had not said, and especially by the odd fact that Lady Forester was here at the George and Dragon.

Lady Forester, he concluded, was at this very moment on her way to Pomfret Priory. Miss Forester had clearly not informed her parent of her whereabouts. Foolish, he knew, because now questions would be asked, and he hoped that answers could be found that might protect the girl. If Lady Forester got her daughter into her control again, Lottie would never hear the end of scolding about her flight. And certainly if word got out concerning the circumstances of her last few weeks, her chances of a respectable marriage, even a respectable spinsterhood if that were her wish, would vanish overnight.

The long and short of it was that Marcus wanted to marry Miss Forester, regardless of her fortune. He did not wish to marry her to save her reputation, and care must be taken not to give Charlotte that notion.

All his wishes would go whistling down the wind if anyone found out about these two weeks. He could take steps to protect her in that regard, but there was nothing he could do about the time she had spent with Sir Albin Drysdale, for he did not know what had transpired between them. Nor, to be blunt, did he know what might have happened to her here at the George and Dragon before tonight.

It was getting darker, and soon he could begin to work his way toward obtaining his rig. For reasons he considered obvious, he did not wish to confront either the landlord, whose kitchen boy he had just abducted, or Lady Forester, whose daughter he had ruined in the eyes of society.

His thoughts ranged over Charlotte's rejection of him at Pentstable. How dreadful had been the days after he had returned to London, under the impression that even a stranger could not abide the thought of marrying him!

But she too had suffered. She had been harried from pillar to post and back. If they could come out of this coil, they could make up for lost time, so to speak. They would marry at once, and still the voice of scandal. Supposing, of course, that she did not turn him down again, thinking he offered only to save her reputation.

The days on the road had revealed to him a gentle, intelligent lady with a mischievous sense of humor and a kindly nature. How much better he would have done for himself had he known her before he had arrived, disastrously, at Pentstable!

He might have made a better showing, although he was realistic enough to know that it would have taken months of gently advancing acquaintance to reach the same regard for each other that a few anonymous days on the road had accomplished.

A warm glow routed the icy chill that had remained like a rock somewhere in the region of his stomach since that first moment when he recognized Lady Forester. The look in Lottie's eyes tonight bore no resemblance to that rejection!

She was far from being the timid, submissive lady her mother thought she was. But neither was he the conventional gentleman he had thought *he* was.

Ah, well, together they had made a tangled skein, and only a sympathetic Providence could make it all right!

20

MARCUS KNEW where he was, at least geographically.

He had returned to the lane where he left Lottie—he must remember to call her Viola until all was cleared up! —to find her curled up like a child on the grassy bank, sound asleep. He watched her for a few moments, feeling a tenderness for her that was new and strange to him.

They might well have a hard way just ahead. Scandal lay in wait for them, and probably there would be lies told and spread abroad, not all of them by others. There would be a few judicious untruths told by him and, if he could persuade Lady Forester to agree, by her as well.

He remembered that shocked expression on the lady's face only a short while ago, and truly he could not blame her, for Lottie, her hair short and ragged, did not appear even female, to say nothing of being recognizable as Miss Forester of Pentstable!

He chuckled, and the small sound brought Lottie wide awake. The moon was nearing the full, and rose soon after sunset. There would be light at least for a while to travel by, although a darkness in the western sky indicated that another of the seasonal storms might be approaching.

Once again he helped her into his curricle, once more he climbed up in his familiar place beside her, and they started off.

"Where are we going?" asked Lottie after they had been on the road for some time.

He knew where he wanted to go. He longed to drive up to Gresham Manor and introduce her as the new Mrs. North. And, God willing, he would do just that. But not tonight.

Knowing he hesitated too long, he blurted out the first thing that came to his mind. "Do you care much?"

She glanced at him in surprise. He looked unwontedly serious, she thought. Her new confidence ebbed away. She believed he had a regard for her, for had he not come to the George and Dragon to find her? He had promised to tell her how he had traced her, but the fact remained that he had not as yet done any such thing.

She knew she was being unfair—there had not been time even for her to explain how it was that she had come to a temporary halt at the George and Dragon. But old habits take time to die.

It was entirely possible, thought the young Miss Forester carefully kept in her subordinate place for long years by her mother, that he had arrived only by happenstance, and had not been looking for her at all. After all, why should a handsome gentleman, no matter how many signs he had given of interest in her, come to seek out a kitchen boy, a gutter-child, above all a young person pursued across England for reasons of which this man was ignorant?

Feeling snubbed, tears stinging behind her eyelids, she leaned back against the seat. Really, she did not care much where they were going. Pomfret receded in her mind until it seemed like a dream. Certainly they were not, as far as she knew, on the direct road to Pomfret. As proof, she knew for a fact that they had not even entered the outskirts of Castleton! And where else was there for her to go?

She was very tired. The short nap while she waited for him to return had only made her sleepier. She drifted into a fitful doze, where kitchen floors rose to the ceiling and shouted for cleaning, Sir Albin's face appeared unaccountably out of a hot oven, and she moved in an alien world, hampered by fetters on her ankles.

The motion of the vehicle caused her to lean on Marcus' shoulder, to his great satisfaction, but there remained something wrong in her dream. At length, a sudden rut in the road jolted her totally awake.

"You didn't answer," she said accusingly. "That was what was wrong."

"I don't know what you mean. I heard no question, unless you refer to your query about our destination."

She shook her head impatiently. "No, no, in the dream. You came into the kitchen, and I asked you . . . What did I ask? I don't remember."

Seizing the idea she had unknowingly presented to him, he said, "Do you think it is significant for a person to appear in another's dream?"

Warned perhaps by a new note in his voice, she parried his suggestion. "I should tell you that that man you leveled at the inn was also in my dream."

"Damn him!"

"He probably will be," she said reasonably.

"You never told me," he said daringly, "why he was after you."

"Do you think I carried off his mother's silver? Where would I carry it? Besides, he's probably already sold it all. Not for the money, but to spite her."

"Why am I not surprised? He is a distinctly ill-bred lout."

"Exactly," she agreed enthusiastically. "Miss W . . . that is, someone whom I know said the family had very recently been in trade."

She was still keeping her own counsel, he saw with some dismay. He had hoped that, since they had been through so much together, she might have decided to confide in him. He had believed her, correctly as it happened, on the verge of telling him everything when that wheel came loose, and he had not only failed to receive her confidences but also lost the girl herself. He did not wish to dwell on the thoughts that kept him company during those days of searching.

But he wished she would talk to him now. He did not know how to broach the subject of marriage to her without coming to grips with their identities, and in so doing, she might well take a view of their circumstances that he did not favor.

She was proud; he knew that. But was she too proud to accept his offer, believing it to be only a reputation-saving suggestion? If she had fled from him at Pentstable, would she vanish from his sight now? She was the woman he wanted to marry, and her property be damned. But he could not offer marriage to her until she confided her identity to him.

It was a dilemma—one that he could not solve.

However, another dilemma was coming fast upon him, but he could take steps toward lessening its consequences. The moon had now risen toward the zenith. The journey to Pomfret, and Gresham of course, required only half a day—or half a night, as was the present case. He had not pushed his cattle, seeing no reason to arrive at Pomfret—and he intended to take her to Pomfret willy-nilly—at an hour well before sunrise.

The crescent moon showed him the rising bank of clouds, and now he could see flashes of lightning in the depths of the bulging storm. A stiff little breeze rose without warning, and it was plain that the storm would break upon them within the hour.

"I think we had best look for shelter. Not under a tree, of course."

"Is there perhaps a town?" she asked. "I have

developed a great dislike of haymows. It seems I've lived most of the past month too close to horses.''

"I'm sorry. I know this country quite well, and there is not an inn between here and . . . at any rate, anywhere close enough to serve."

He peered across the head bobbing in front of them, trying to catch sight of a landmark or two. He knew a building ahead that would be most suitable for shelter. Unfortunately, it was another barn. Once he and his Viola had won through this crisis, he would never again allow her to visit a stable. Except, of course, their own.

The wind whipped up into a half-gale, tossing branches up and down and driving the horses into rolling-eyed fright. Marcus caught sight of the barn he was looking for, and the curricle turned off the narrow road into a narrower drive that led to the barn, just as the first huge drops of rain fell.

Giving the reins to Lottie to hold, he dashed through the downpour to open the doors. Lottie drove the curricle in—the first time she had held reins in her hands since that wild drive away from Albin's ambush—and Marcus closed the doors behind them.

They were in a fairly small barn, clearly one for storage on outer boundaries of an estate. There were no other buildings around that she could see in the short time she waited for Marcus to open the doors, and she deemed it likely that no one would disturb them this night.

Marcus tended to the horses, putting them in a stall and forking hay down to them. Lottie helped rub them down. How strange it was that horses, so much stronger than humans, yet needed such great care. Nobody rubbed her down when she was caught in a rainstorm!

The haymow still held the heat of the day. As weary as she was of spending her nights in the company of horses, she was grateful for the shelter. Overhead, the rain drummed on the roof like thundering hooves, and there was lightning from time to time.

Had she sought a time of the year that was the most unpropitious for traveling like a Gypsy, she could not have done better than this rainy early summer. The few days of sunshine had not coincided with her journeying, but instead had come when she was at the George and Dragon, scrubbing floors, cleaning bedrooms.

She heard footsteps on the ladder. *He* was coming. She had no name to call him but for the fantastical Sebastian, and somehow that name served no longer. She had entered upon a new aspect of their friendship, and although she was not experienced enough to be sure, she suspected that it was in the hope of this kind of affection, of respect, of great ease of mind in his company, that she had refused even to meet Marcus North. Now she had this kind of feeling, but she did not know whether he returned it.

He followed her up the ladder to the haymow. The hay was new, and he judged had been mowed no more than a week ago. "The first thing," he said as they stood knee-deep in the fragrant dry grass, "is to take off those wet clothes of yours."

With spirit she answered, "What would I wear otherwise? I had not the time to pack a bandbox, you will recall."

"At least you must take off that smock," he told her. "You'll catch your death. I'll give you my shirt."

"No."

"Do you fear me?" he asked, surprised and, knowing his own intentions to be honorable, insulted. "You need not, you know. I have no wish to watch you undress," he lied, "but I do not wish to nurse a feverish la . . . *person* all day tomorrow."

"I shall not require nursing," she said as stiffly as he.

He regarded her with exasperation. Finally he agreed. "All right, I'll go down and leave you alone. But you must promise me to take off those wet clothes."

She hesitated, clearly considering the suggestion. She had won, of course, but she had gained a hollow victory. Suddenly the haymow seemed a lonely place, to lie in solitary grandeur while her good friend found a place below with the livestock. She could not think how to answer him without seeming forward. Fortunately she saw him shiver in a sudden gust of wind coming through a crack in the wall.

"You are as wet as I am," she said with a small laugh. "I think we must make the best of it. There's plenty of room for us both."

"So there is," he said, making no effort to move in the far reaches of the hay. He knelt beside her and pulled hay over to cover her up. She was at once much warmer.

Without invitation, he lay down, not close, but near enough to reach out and touch her cheek with the back of his hand.

"Are you comfortable?"

"Yes, I am. Even this is better than a good many places I have been in recently."

"You never told me about them," said Marcus. "Not even where you stayed those nights you vanished from my sight. Why would you not let me pay for your lodging?"

"Such an arrangement," she said in a shocked voice, "would have been totally ineligible."

"Any well-brought-up young lady would agree," he said. "But I thought that perhaps you might have trusted me? You surely know I would do nothing against your wishes."

"I know," she said. But the trouble was, she thought, that what she wished for was quite ineligible too. What did she want? She was not thinking of marriage, surely, even though the thought stuck in her mind like a chestnut bur? She might have had her chance at that, but turned it down. And she would not admit that perhaps her immediate wishes had nothing to do with wedlock, but only with the comfortable presence of the man she could no longer think of as a brother, that presence that had something very odd to do with her breathing.

It was as though she stepped too close to the edge of a cliff. She remembered a visit to the seashore when she was much younger. Standing on the brink, where the earth fell away to rocks far below, she had felt this same dizziness, as though the sea crashing among the rocks below called to her to take that fatal step.

So it was now—and she suspected that the step she longed to take now, to reach out to this man who had become dear to her, and risk what would happen next, would be as disastrous as it would have been stepping off the cliff into nothing but air.

Instinctively she pulled back.

And, instinctively, she closed her eyes and appeared to sleep. After a long moment she heard him lie back on the soft hay and sigh once, deeply. In a moment, feigned sleep became real, and she heard no more of the storm outside, nor was she torn for the moment by her inner tempest.

The morning had not been far away when they had fallen asleep. Too soon the light struck Lottie's eyelids and she woke with a start. It had been a long time since she had opened her eyes to surroundings that were familiar. Nor was this morning any exception.

She summoned up recollections of yesterday, the George and Dragon, the arrival of Sir Albin and . . . Sebastian! And she remembered with hot cheeks that he had lain beside her all night. How could she have allowed it!

It came to her, even before she turned her head, that

she was alone. He had left her there, asleep, and gone
. . . Gone?

Propriety was banished from her mind. She needed
him, and not only for his help, his transportation, his
protection. It struck her like a blow. She—independent,
plain, unattractive Charlotte Forester—needed *him*!

Suddenly fearing he had left her, she scrambled
across the haymow toward the edge of the loft, on
hands and knees. She heard the trampling of the horses,
and their odd snuffling noises indicating that a human
was nearby.

She looked over the edge. Just inside the door to her
right stood the curricle, shafts to the ground. The horses
were still stalled. And Sebastian had not left her.

Her new friend was standing directly below her, his
back to her. Something about him set up echoes in her
mind. Somewhere she had seen, from just this same
angle . . .

It was as though a large brass gong had sounded in
her head, sending reverberations throughout her body.
She could not think for the clamor. She could only stare
down at the bent head of the man who had become so
necessary to her peace of mind—that same bent head,
and broad shoulders, and beguiling little curl at the nape
of the neck that she had seen from the stair railing at
Pentstable.

She had traveled day after day in the company of a
man who pursued her, not for evil intent like Sir Albin,
she must suppose, but certainly with the same degree of
dogged persistence. After all, Pomfret was clearly worth
something to him!

She could not fathom how he came upon her on a
road where no one knew her, but she would put nothing
past him.

She had refused even to see Marcus North, and yet he
was here with her, his identity kept as secret as hers! She
loathed him!

She must have made a small strangled sound, for he turned at once and looked up at her. He saw an ashen face with great green eyes glaring at him under that ridiculously chopped hair.

"Good God, what is it? What happened? Was there" —he swallowed swiftly—"a snake in the hay?"

"You . . . you . . ." She stopped and closed her eyes. Taking a deep breath, she started over. With icy words, not melted even by the heat of her angry sense of betrayal, she told him precisely what had happened.

"Did not my mother tell you that I did not wish even to see you? I believe I asked her also to inform you that, under certain circumstances, I might *sell* Pomfret Priory to you, since that was your goal. At least Lady Monteagle certainly hinted as much!"

Appalled, he forgot himself. "Charlotte—"

"So, you *do* know my name. That silly *Twelfth Night* fable. Did you think I was stupid enough to be beguiled by it?" Never mind that she had indeed been enchanted by it! "I wonder that you did not falter once and call me by my own name. But you had enough at stake to make the care worthwhile, of course."

"Lottie, I do not want—"

" 'Miss Forester,' please! Don't touch me," she warned sharply as he moved to the ladder. "Don't come near me or . . . or I'll jump!"

He assessed her mood correctly, and hastily stepped back to the ground. "We can discuss this," he said with hope. "I can explain everything."

"Ha!"

"But I'm getting a crick in my neck. Come on down, my dear. I won't touch you. But you're wrong, you know. I did not know who you were."

She perched on the top of the ladder. Indignant as she was, and with reason, she was conscious of a stream of betrayal from within that she must put a stop to. True, he had misled her. But also true, he might well have an explanation.

He had not harmed her, and indeed had taken the greatest care of her. And worst of all, she felt a strong pull toward him, even now, looking down at his perfidious face.

"No explanation is possible," she said on a calmer, almost mournful note. "You wanted Pomfret, and the only way you could see was to marry me. But that didn't work, so you devised this dastardly scheme."

"Lottie . . . pray forgive me, Miss Forester, you couldn't be more mistaken!"

"Then, pray, tell me why you took up with a grimy stableboy. You knew all the time who I was!"

"Lottie," said Marcus, remembering the grubby child he had found first hiding in a ditch, "how could anyone have known that Miss Forester would ever appear . . ." He gestured, feeling the futility of his situation. "Like that," he finished lamely.

There was some truth to what he said, she acknowledged. If it were possible he did not know her at first, however, and gave shelter, as it were, to a lad in need, that action was admirable.

But sometime he had discovered who she was, and he had not told her so.

"When did you find out my name?" she asked in an altered voice.

Encouraged, he told her quickly, "Not until last night."

Her memory of last night was tinged with color both rosy and warm. "Last night?"

Not privy to her thoughts, he explained. "When I saw your mother at the George. It all came together then. I recalled that you had left Pentstable, to my mortification. I could think of no reason for her to be traveling in this part of the country unless she was looking for you at Pomfret."

"Ah," she said. It was a long and mournfully drawn-out sigh, and Marcus realized he had lost what sympathy she had for him. "I thought once that Pomfret would be a haven for me, a place where I could go and no one would trouble me. Not my mother, wanting me to marry a perfect stranger—oh, yes, she did speak of marriage!—nor Sir Albin, attempting my virtue again. And especially not Mr. Marcus North, who was so eager for my property he could not wait to meet me in London!"

It was impossible to ignore the contempt in her voice when she spoke of him, and he did not try. He was not weary in the same way that she was, but the strain of the past days had not been hers alone. He had dealt with his altering emotions and with the thought that he was not the prosaic, plodding carthorse of a figure, but was indeed capable of mounting a knightly white steed and rescuing his lady.

And now the worst of all blows: the lady, even as rescued, spurned him.

The tight rein he had held on his tongue all these days, lest he frighten her away, and, these last hours, lest he reveal his sudden knowledge prematurely, slipped.

"Let me tell you, Miss Forester," he said, so angry his voice was all but inaudible, "that of all the ungrateful minxes I have ever seen—"

The words had no sooner left his lips than he knew he had made a grave mistake. She pounced on his error. "Ungrateful? I should not like to treat true kindness with contempt. But I must say that gratitude in the circumstances is not applicable. You wish to own Pomfret, either by marriage or by purchase. I see no reason for gratitude."

"You . . . exasperating . . . female!" he said, his voice taut. "I want to marry you, and to hell with Pomfret. I can't seem to make you understand: Pomfret means nothing to me." Honesty should have demanded he add

the word "now," but there was a time and a place for
honesty, neither of which was present.

He turned on his heel and started to put his horses to
the shafts. Opening the door, he backed the curricle out
and turned it, ready to start back the way they had
come.

She did not want to see him go, but she could not bear
his presence for another minute. Just the same, she
hurried across the barn floor to stand in the open door.

He paused just before he touched the whip to the
horses' rumps. Calling down to her, he informed her,
"Go out to the road this way and turn right."

"Why?"

"That's the short way to Pomfret Priory."

She looked at him, astonished. "So close?"

"You spent the night in your own barn." He
hesitated as though to renew the quarrel, but then
thought better of it.

"I must have sent you on alone in any event," he
informed her. "It would have been hard to explain my
presence to old Miss Granville. Your cousin who lives
there, you know."

"I did not know you knew," she said in a small voice.

"Perhaps you will convince her of your identity. Certainly Miss Forester will be hard to recognize in those
clothes. I swear to you I did not." Then, setting the
horses down the drive, he glanced back for a moment,
and wished he hadn't.

Never in the world, he thought, had there ever been
such a forlorn figure, shoulders drooping, pathetic in
the extreme. He almost turned around.

But why should he feel sorry for her? She had chosen
Pomfret Priory rather than him. She was standing on
her own ground, the lady proudly on her property. And
he? He was driving fast toward the monastic comfort of
Gresham Manor, as unhappy as he had ever been.

21

LOTTIE APPROACHED the front entrance of Pomfret Priory as in a dream. She had never seen it, but she had heard her grandmother describe it so thoroughly that she believed she could move through the rooms blindfolded.

She trudged, numbed with shock, up the long winding driveway now. The revelation that she had traveled with Marcus North, the man she never wanted even to meet, had stunned her. So had his informing her that her mother had arrived at the George and Dragon the night before, and neither lady had seen the other.

But the most distressing thought of all was one she must learn to put away on a shelf somewhere at the back of her mind, for she could not bear yet to look at it in the blinding light of reality.

She had fallen in love with the one man—save for Sir Albin!—she would not, could not marry. The man who loved her house and fields, the man who had appeared kind, thoughtful, a joyous companion—that same man who was now revealed to be merely a fortune hunter.

How narrow an escape she had had!

But she was not sure, would in all likelihood never know, whether she wanted to escape or not.

She stood at the last curve of the driveway and looked at her new home. Priory was surely a misnomer, she thought, until she saw at the far left corner of the house a sort of square tower that could, if one allowed his imagination to roam, take on the appearance of an ancient priory bell tower, since ruined and rebuilt by one of the ancestral Granvilles.

It would help the illusion, she thought, when viewed through an early-morning fog.

A comfortable-looking house, she agreed, but one to lose a husband over? Not quite!

It did not occur to her to take stock of her appearance and then travel to the kitchen door and announce her arrival. Her attitude of mind automatically went back to the days at Pentstable, when she was Miss Lottie, cosseted by the servants and as confident of her position in the world as could be.

Gone were the days of "Miss Wythe" and the toil-some days of "John Tyson, kitchen boy." It was as though a curtain, opaque and immovable, had dropped between her life to this point and the future.

The only reality now was that journey through the halcyon days of early summer, a bright memory to comfort her in the drear days ahead.

Reaching the front door, she lifted the brass knocker —well-polished, she noted—and let it fall. The woman who opened the door to her presented an unfriendly face.

"What is it? We don't take beggars here, boy. Nor go to the back door, either, unless you're willing to work for your bread and cheese."

The door started to close before Lottie found her tongue. "But I'm not a beggar—that is, I'm not a boy." Speech was so difficult, so inadequate! She put out a hand to stop the door from slamming shut. "I am Miss Forester."

"You don't say! And I'm the Queen of the May."

"Really, I am—"

From within came a voice, old and slightly cracked, but it brought hope to Lottie. "Who is it, Mrs. Winston? One of the neighbors?"

"A nasty boy the likes of a chimney sweep, ma'am."

Mrs. Winston turned her head to answer her mistress, and Lottie took advantage. She pushed forward, crossing the threshold into the entrance hall, brushing past the woman, and raising her voice.

"Cousin Evaline?"

She was answered immediately.

Emerging from a room at the left of the hall was the elderly Miss Granville. Lottie heard a muffled "Lord Amighty" from the housekeeper, but she ignored the woman.

Cousin Evaline was obviously a Granville. Tall, angular, just like Grandmother, thought Lottie, and felt a rush of affection for her. She looked into her cousin's hazel eyes, clear as a girl's, and watched a look of wonder come over the strong features.

"Good God," said Cousin Evaline with force, "you're Adelia Granville, to the life!"

In a moment she was enfolded in Evaline's embrace, dirty clothes and all, and to her embarrassment, she began to sob. "There, there," soothed Evaline, patting her shoulder, then speaking in quite a different tone to Mrs. Winston.

"Can't you see the girl needs something to eat, I'll be bound. And these rags . . . Is there anything that will fit her? And I wouldn't wonder if she's been through some adventures that, please God, we will never know about, and we may consider ourselves fortunate if that mother of hers isn't close behind!"

"You sound like Grandmother," said Lottie bewilderedly when she could stifle her sobs long enough to speak. Her smile was watery but full of present contentment. She had come home.

The next morning, after a sinfully luxurious bath followed by a sleep as deep as a well, Lottie dressed her-

self in borrowed clothes once more. Those she tried on
at first were old-fashioned and somewhat too big for
her, for she had not her grandmother's height, but at
least they were feminine.

"Did Grandmother really wear this?"

Lottie was standing in the middle of Evaline's sitting
room upstairs, while Tessie carefully dropped her
grandmother's gown over her head. The yellow silk,
cracked with age, still held the faint aroma of the
lavender in which it had been put away.

Lottie looked down at herself. The dress was
fashioned with a tight waist, with side panniers to
accentuate the slender curve above the hips.

"Look at this," she laughed ruefully, tracing with her
fingers the stiffened cloth meant to cup a full bosom. "I
look so *stupid* in this."

"You look like a boy," agreed Evaline, "and doubtless that's what saved you these last weeks." She had
heard a sketchy account of Lottie's adventures, and
clucked over her fondly, admired her courage and good
fortune and cleverness, and said nothing about their
neighbor Mr. North, for the simple reason that Lottie
had not seen fit to mention him.

Then she was required to try on several other of her
grandmother's gowns—a *robe à la polonaise,* all ruffles
and flounces and panniers. There were others.

"Adelia always had new gowns. I don't think she
wore a ball gown more than once. I was fortunate
enough to be nearly as tall, although not so graceful,
and I inherited many a gown that needed only a bit of
alteration." She regarded Lottie thoughtfully. "Do you
know, I do not quite visualize you in a *robe à la
circassienne,* or a *robe à la lévité*—"

"What on earth could that be—a gown to *laugh* in?"

"No, my dear. Simply a gown to flirt in."

"Grandmother was a flirt, I suppose?"

"Your grandmother," said Evaline with sudden firmness, "was not a great beauty. Not like your mother, whom I remember well although I have not seen her for twenty years, but a woman of enormous distinction. And such charm and presence. She had real presence, like royalty. She never entered a room unnoticed. She danced every dance at every ball we attended, for you must know that we went together to many events."

"I never knew she was such a belle."

"And you, my dear, are so much like her I gasped when I first laid eyes on you. A lady of great distinction, I promise you."

"And you think I am like her?"

"The very image, believe me." Evaline did not overlook the girl's wistful glance. Probably she had been told she was not pretty, for she wasn't, at least in the conventional sense. But there had been nothing conventional about Adelia Granville, and Evaline suspected that Lottie bore the same stamp.

"But I will admit," Evaline continued, "that I am longing to throw away those motley garments you wore when you arrived."

In the event, Lottie wore none of her grandmother's clothes. Instead, Evaline agreed that too many alterations would be needed before she could venture downstairs without breaking her neck on the skirts. Evaline plundered her own wardrobe to provide a round gown of muslin for mornings and a slightly more elaborate dress for evenings.

That first day at Pomfret stretched, so Lottie thought, interminably. She found regrettably that every time she sat down to rest for a moment, she dropped off to sleep.

"Tired, that's what you are, child," said Evaline, fussing over her. "And starving too, I judge."

"Thank you for taking me in so kindly."

"What else could I do for Adelia's granddaughter? Besides, I feel we are destined to be great friends." Without an obvious correlation, she added, "Shall we expect your mother to come soon?"

Lottie shook her head. "I truly do not know. She was at that inn I told you about, but she did not see me. So I do not know, but I should judge she was on her way here, wouldn't you think?"

"I do indeed," Evaline said dryly. She had shared Adelia's dislike for Lottie's mother, but she saw no reason to tell Lottie so. Sufficient unto the day, she thought—time enough when the present Lady Forester darkened the front door.

In the event, Lady Forester was not the first visitor to come to Pomfret after Lottie's arrival.

At the sound of wheels on the drive, Lottie's first thought did not include her mother. She ran to the window overlooking the drive.

He's come! she thought at first. Sebas . . . that is, Marcus North has come. To apologize, certainly . . . to explain, possibly . . . or even just to see her again, not likely.

But she would not be caught at the window, watching out like any kitchen maid for her follower. She hurried back to her chair, and smiled at Evaline. "A curricle," she informed the old lady, "and therefore not my mother."

"Lady Forester driving a curricle? *That* I should like to see," Evaline said wryly.

Floyd, the footman, in due time announced the visitor.

"Sir Albin Drysdale," he said, breathless with the honor. Pomfret was not in the ordinary way of entertaining gentlemen of elegance.

"What!"

"My dear, is he. . . ?"

Sir Albin was in the room. His impatience was like a live thing, menacing, like a dog with a growl in its throat.

"Ah, Miss . . . Forester! My compliments, ma'am." On his best behavior, he bowed to Evaline.

"What are you doing here?" Lottie demanded. She had risen to receive her guest, and stood unmoving. She glared at him in a way he might not have expected. But Lottie was on her home ground, and was not inclined to truckle to anyone, let alone this bully who had caused her a good deal of trouble.

"I came," said Sir Albin, nothing daunted by her reception of him, "to see whether you had taken any hurt in the accident."

"Accident! Do you mean that cowardly sabotage on the wheel? That was no accident. We could all have been killed by your villainy."

"Good God!" exclaimed Sir Albin. "Don't tell me you were riding in that curricle?"

"Very well, I shall not."

"Then North knew all the time who you were? I'll call him out for that! He lied to me."

"No more," said Lottie without a clear idea of what Sir Albin was talking about, "than you have lied to everyone. Can you deny that it was your false witness that caused me to be dismissed by your mother?"

Miss Evaline Granville had not enjoyed herself quite so much since the time five years ago when young Willy Dennis, a terror to anyone within a radius of ten miles who crossed him, had come up against the Fat Man at the village fair, and had fought him for a wheel of cheese. Of course, Willy ended up on his back, and he was well-served at that. Evaline had to disguise her interest in watching the fisticuffs that day. But here she was now, in her own parlor, or rather dear Lottie's parlor, and had no need to conceal her excitement.

Physically, these combatants were ill-matched, but she would wager, were she a gambling woman, on the small figure standing defiantly two yards away.

Sir Albin snorted. "I had no need to lie," he told them. "My stepmother does not go against my wishes."

"Of course not," accused Lottie. "She is afraid of you. I should like you to know, sir, that I do not bid you welcome. I think you had better leave at once."

"I think, Miss Forester, that you and I have things to discuss that you would prefer to keep private."

Sir Albin sent a speaking glance at the older woman. Suddenly Evaline's amusement turned to alarm. There was a look in his eyes that was meant to turn her veins to water, and while she did not fear him, not *precisely*, she noticed that Lottie had paled.

"My cousin—" Lottie began.

"Your cousin," interrupted Evaline, "will leave you alone. However, my dear, I shall not be far away should you need me."

Once alone, Sir Albin seemed to remember that he intended to be affable, and not indulge in his usual menacing ways of dealing. "Pray be seated, Miss Forester."

"How do you know who I am, Sir Albin?"

"Your mother made inquiries, after that masquerade of yours. It might be more proper for me now to address myself to your mother, but since you are removed from her protection, and for various other reasons, I choose to speak directly to you."

"Various other reasons? What may they be?"

"I do wish you would be seated. We would be more comfortable together."

"You will be leaving very soon, I suspect."

"It does occur to me," he continued, "that you might not wish your mother to hear all the reasons for our betrothal. And believe me, I shall take no joy in spreading such truths in places where I know rumors always receive a warm welcome."

Shakily she reached behind her for the arm of a chair, and with its support sat down. Her voice trembled. "Did I hear the word 'betrothal'?"

"Indeed you did. I shall obtain a special license, and I am sure you will agree with me that we wish a private ceremony—"

"Get out!"

"Come now, is that any way—"

"Believe me, Sir Albin," she said, her voice throbbing with anger barely suppressed, "I shall not marry you. Never. Not if you were the last man on earth—"

"As I probably am, for you," he interrupted smoothly. "At least, you may as well put away any hopes you have of marrying, as soon as word spreads that you have been traveling through the country, in as havey-cavey a manner as the saddest romp might do, alone in company only with a man who—"

"You cannot believe anyone would credit you."

"And why not? Your Mr. North could certainly not deny it. Nor are you safe with your own secret. If you recall, you gave yourself away as soon as I mentioned that accident." His grin became wolfish. "I meant, of course, the accident at the bridge, where the horse ran away with you. I feared you had lost your memory, you know, for you did not appear in any of your likely haunts."

Guilt, striking unaware, has a debilitating influence on one's determination to resist. But nonetheless she allowed her real indignation to appear. She stood up. "I asked you before to leave, Sir Albin. Now I demand that you do so. You are not welcome now or ever in my home."

She took a step toward him, but he did not stir from his chair. Instead he reached to grab her wrist and pull her closer to him.

"Come now, Charlotte, don't fight. We'll make a fine pair."

His eyes glittered, and she shrank away from him. "Let me go!"

It was that business in the woods all over again. Only now there was no small Puff to save her. There was no time to think, or even to scream. She could only resist to the limit of her strength, for he was rapidly overcoming her. He was out of the chair, trying to hold her hand away from his face, and at the same time lifting her from her feet.

She kicked once, and, feeling her toe touch some part of him, kicked again, this time with all the force she could summon. Once again her luck was in. Her toe found the newly healed wound on the calf of his leg, the wound in the shape of Puff's teeth, and the pain caused him to lose his grip on her.

"You she-devil!"

"I think," came a clear voice, elderly and cracked but strong with authority, "it is time for you to take your leave, Sir Albin."

Rubbing his throbbing calf with one hand, he turned his attention to the old lady, who had no business, he thought, to interrupt him. She stood inside the room, away from the door to the hall. Behind her, through the open door, could be seen, ranged in a formidable row, three rather formidably stocky men wearing expressions that boded no good for Sir Albin.

He stood up, and contemplated the men with dawning understanding. Much as he hated to, for the first time in his life he was forced to admit defeat. Not only did he give up the field at the moment, considering that he was doomed to failure in winning the heiress in marriage, but he also recognized he had lost in the second part of his goal.

No revenge would be wreaked on Miss Forester, not while those sturdy men were so close at hand and ready.

She was protected as no governess should be. And while she had driven him to pursue her the way he had never pursued a female before, the game was, to put it briefly, not worth the candle.

He did not leave with good grace, however. He spoke to her one last time, one final thrust of venom-tipped words.

"If you think your friend North will come up to the mark, let me tell you, you could not be more mistaken. The man is not eligible for marriage."

She could not refrain from questioning him. Not eligible? Impossible!

"What do you mean?" she whispered.

His only answer was a grin of sheer malice. Then, escorted unobtrusively by the farm men that Evaline had summoned, he was gone.

Not eligible for marriage? Marcus North? Impossible! she thought again. He had called with purpose at Pentstable, had he not? And if Lady Monteagle had considered him eligible then, he had surely been eligible then, so why was he not now?

She had completely lost sight of the fact that she had rejected him then, and had in fact made no secret of her loathing for him only yesterday. What difference did it truly make to her whether there were impediments to his marriage or not?

It made a difference.

Just how, she was not sure. But forget about whether Marcus North had come to Pentstable, all the while knowing any offer he might make could not be valid, for some obstacle only he knew.

The Forester attorneys would soon have made a mockery of any such offer, did such fraud exist. No, Lottie concluded, at that time Marcus had been an eligible suitor. But also, now she remembered that somewhere in the midst of that quarrel in the barn—accusations thrown and returned, anger and hurt rising like a high tide to overwhelm them both—there had been made a small remark that she had overlooked at the time.

She could not recall the precise words, but the remark stayed with her like the sweet kernel of a nut within a hard shell.

"Cousin Evaline, do you know how to get to Gresham Manor?"

"Of course, although I have not visited there recently. May I. . . .? No, I shall not ask why."

It was nearly time to confide in her totally, Lottie believed. She had kept too many secrets recently, had not trusted Sebastian with her confidences. It would have been better for them both had she done so.

But she had not known she would fall in love with him, had she?

"I would tell you, dear Evaline, but I am not sure myself."

Following Evaline's directions, and warning her that if her mother had been recently at the George and Dragon, she would doubtless be on her way to Pomfret at this very hour, Lottie set out on a back lane over the fields and along the edge of some woods on her way to Gresham. She had declined the offer of a vehicle, for she could not be sure that Sir Albin had left the vicinity yet. It would be the height of folly to drive out on the public road with only a maid or a footman, and put herself at hazard for kidnapping, or worse.

But what would she say to Marcus North when she arrived, always assuming that he would allow her in the house? "Are you an eligible suitor?" That would not do. "Can we not be friends?" She didn't want him to be her friend.

That was not true—he was probably her best friend

ever. But she wanted to be more, much more. And how did a well-brought-up lady indicate to a gentleman that she was agreeable to receive his advances?

Well-brought-up lady—that was the key. Marcus wanted a lady for Gresham Manor, and Lottie the Gypsy had been an unpleasant revelation to him. Her mission to Gresham was doomed at the start!

And yet, there had been something he said . . .

She traversed the field, crossed a stile that Cousin Evaline had said was the boundary line, and entered Gresham land before she remembered what he had said, the sweet kernel that she had almost forgotten.

"To hell with Pomfret," he had said. But before that: "I want to marry you."

And *that* was why she was on her way to Gresham Manor!

22

THE BACK lane to Gresham debouched from a small but ancient woods onto the west lawn of the manor. Lottie paused for a moment to consider her next move.

The front of the house lay ahead of her to the right, and she took a few steps in that direction. Then she saw the curricle standing before the entrance, a curricle she had seen only an hour or so before.

Sir Albin Drysdale was here!

She did not want to interrupt that conversation, to be sure! But neither did she want to stand here on the edge of the woods like an unwelcome guest afraid to demand entry at the house.

Her need to talk to Marcus precluded going back to Pomfret and writing a letter, for example, or taking this back road at another time. Besides, she thought it might be wise to be on hand to deny whatever Sir Albin chose to say to Marcus about her.

Thus, hesitating, she was a spectator to the next development. Of course she knew that Marcus and Albin shared a vibrant feeling of ill-will. One would not look lightly upon a man who for sheer malice loosened a wheel and broke Irving's leg, after all.

Nor would that culprit, being of villainous nature to begin with, take kindly to being leveled in an innyard, nor for that matter, wearing a fading red whip mark.

But, knowing all that, she was still stunned witless when she saw the side door of Gresham Manor open and two men emerge, each carrying a weapon of some kind. She was not conversant with dueling pistols, but she suspected that she soon might become so.

They couldn't be planning to fight a duel! There were no seconds. The duel as an instrument of unhallowed justice was illegal. And surely Marcus would not indulge in such an outrageous escapade!

But she had proof of his metal, and she now accepted without question that a duel was about to take place. Quickly she stepped behind a large tree trunk, to think what to do. She could make her presence known, and the duelists would in all likelihood halt. But what next?

She froze where she was. There was something odd about the way Sir Albin walked, looking around him as though to reassure himself the two were alone. He was up to something, she decided as she peered out from her sheltering tree trunk.

In a moment, her doubts were resolved. The men paced off a certain distance, faced each other. How could Marcus lend himself to this idiotic affair? She dared not call out to warn him, lest she distract him fatally. She could only watch in silent horror.

The word came clearly to her: "One!" She could not tell which of the men was calling the count. "Two!"

And while she held her breath, waiting for the count of "Three!", she saw the shot. First a puff of smoke—from Albin's gun!—and then the sound of the explosion.

Marcus fell, slowly, like a tree toppling, taking forever to reach the ground. Wounded, or dead, by the hand of a man who had shot to kill on the second count, before there was any chance of himself being wounded. And the deed done without witnesses!

Save for herself!

She heard someone screaming as she launched herself out of the woods and across the lawn, and knew the sound came from her own tortured throat as she ran.

Precisely what happened next, and in what order, she was never to know. Albin's face, holding a shocked expression as he caught sight of her, vanished as he turned and ran toward the front of the house, where his curricle stood.

Men poured out of the side door of the house, and a few came running across the lawn from the back. There was a maid who stood screaming, her apron flung up to her face. An older, plump woman emerged, taking in the situation at a glance, and stepped up promptly to deliver a blow to the side of the maid's head that cut off the scream as though with a knife.

And Lottie herself, on the ground, with Marcus' head in her lap, watching the blood oozing out of his chest and the stain spreading ominously across his shirt.

Later, Lottie marveled at the ease with which the staff at Gresham Manor accepted her direction. The doctor was called, and while they waited for him, Marcus was carried upstairs to his own bed.

Lottie made to follow, but Potter, the butler, stopped her.

"Let his man undress him, miss. He'd not know you were there as it is."

"Oh, Potter!" she cried, blinking back the tears that had sprung to her eyes as soon as Marcus was taken upstairs. "Why did he ever agree?"

She was aware that as a question it was not coherent. She did owe them all an explanation, she supposed. She knew that her appearance running across the lawn toward the fallen man might give rise to unhealthy speculation, else.

"It was that visitor, you know," she said on a calmer note. "Sir Albin Drysdale is his name. Did you see him?"

"Yes, miss. He asked for the master. He let his horse stand," Potter continued, his breath stifled by disapproval. "He said he wasn't to stay but a moment. Long enough to kill the master!"

Potter was silent for a moment before adding, "Do you think he meant to *kill* Mr. North?"

"Yes."

"But he has never been here before—that I'll take my oath on. And the master never hurt anyone in his life!"

Her thoughts were entirely engaged on the floor above her head. What was going on up there? Had Marcus already died, and she not with him?

Where was that doctor?

Potter still stood before her, and she realized he was mutely asking questions that she must take care in answering. It would not do to tell Marcus' butler that his master had been engaged in bare-knuckled fighting only a day ago, or that he had traveled in harmony and even delight with a stableboy—rather a kitchen boy, from her last employment!—or that . . .

"I am Miss Charlotte Forester," she told Potter, "of Pomfret Priory. I happened to be standing"—never mind why!—"along the edge of the woods, since I came along the back lane from Pomfret. I saw the whole thing. Sir Albin was not fair. He shot on Two."

Potter seemed relieved. "That explains it, miss. Mr. North is a first-rate shot. And to think that Sir Albin rode away without a scratch!"

Unless Marcus dies, she thought, then there will be murder charged against the man. She was the only witness, however, and females were rarely allowed to speak to the case.

The simple solution came to her full-blown. If Marcus died, and Sir Albin, having taken care to have no witnesses to his foul deed, emerged a free man, she, Charlotte Forester, would track him down and kill him herself!

The doctor came and went away again, shaking his

head. "A chancy thing, never seen the like," he told Lottie. "Another inch to the right and he'd be on his way to the cemetery. As it is, if the fever doesn't get too high, he'll do."

"How long," asked Potter, aware of the difficulties lying in wait for a staff who tried to keep Mr. North immobile, "until he is up and on his feet again?"

The doctor chuckled. "As long as you can keep him down. I judge no more than twenty-four hours. But if he listens to me, he'll stay in bed for a week."

Lottie could not bear to return to Pomfret without a reassuring glimpse of Marcus. The doctor had said he was fine, but Lottie was past the point of taking assurances of whatever nature from anybody.

She went upstairs, Potter trailing anxiously behind. "You were intending to go up as soon as I left, weren't you?" she suggested. "We'll go together."

Potter was not certain of the status of this intimidating lady who was clearly a gentlewoman, though her appearance was, to say the least, startling. A slight figure, barely coming up to the butler's shoulder, without the curves that Potter liked in a female, yet she had a presence that belied her small stature, and a hairstyle—if one could call it a style—the like of which he had never seen.

Potter had been in service at Gresham Manor for a matter of nearly thirty years, ever since young master was an infant. He searched the long halls of his memory, and at last, as they reached the upper floor, he remembered. This bit of a person was old Lady Forester's granddaughter! Now he understood everything!

Miss Adelia, Lady Forester that was, had returned from the south to live from time to time at Pomfret, when she had had her fill, as she said, of that fool Lidia, whom her son had married, to his sorrow. And a great lady the dowager was, too! Potter would be much mistaken if this granddaughter of hers did not turn out to be another such.

Marcus lay ashen and immobile in the huge bed, his eyes closed. However, when he heard her step, he stirred.

"Viola?"

Potter knew very well that Miss Forester's given name was Charlotte, for she had just told him so. His heart sank, as he feared Mr. North was wandering in his mind, but to his surprise, the young lady answered at once, and went to stand beside the bed.

Marcus reached for her hand. Frowning, he said with an effort, "You saw?"

"I did indeed," said Lottie. "How do you feel?"

"Dreadful," he answered swiftly. But Potter thought he looked better from the moment he held Miss Forester's hand.

"Why . . . come?"

She sank to her knees beside the bed, so that her eyes were level with his. "We didn't finish yesterday." He looked a question, and she continued. "You said to hell with Pomfret."

Potter thought this was quite the oddest conversation he had ever heard. He dared not move a muscle, however, lest they remember his presence. It was strange, but it was as though they were speaking in two languages, one the actual words, of course, but the other conveyed in silence through the air. Nonsense, of course, but that was how it seemed to him, and he would never tell anyone, for who would believe such a lunatic idea?

Marcus seemed to be trying to remember. She could tell the exact moment when the rest of that particular sentence came to him, for the focus of his eyes shifted and he gazed intently at her.

"The other . . . you came to finish?"

He was speaking with difficulty now, and she judged the laudanum was taking effect. But she could not let him sink into unconsciousness still not knowing what she had come to tell him.

"The argument, of course. But not an end, I think? Marcus, I should like to say yes—yes, dear Marcus."

The light in his eyes warmed her, illuminated for her the strong bonds that held them. They had both tasted adventure, both in their travels together and in their growing exploration and delight with each other.

It might be long before they set out on the road again, and most likely they would journey conventionally, a traveling coach and four, outriders, perhaps a chariot of servants far enough behind to avoid the clouds of dust. She fancied she could hear the wheels on the gravel drive below, already!

The other journey? The two of them together, taking ever-increasing joy in each other and their love? Life would not be long enough for this.

Marcus spoke again before the opiate overwhelmed him. "No more Sebastian!" he said, to Potter's bewilderment. Then Marcus fell asleep, his hand in hers and a smile on his face. Potter, no fool, might not be able to understand the conversation, but he surely knew a couple in love when he saw one. He stole away quietly, to pass the news to the rest of the household staff that the master was to be leg-shackled at last.

So when Lady Forester, whose coach Lottie had heard on the drive, came into the house, she was greeted with a warmth that surprised her, and news that shocked her.

"Shot? Oh, no, Lottie didn't . . ." She bit her lip. Lottie had run away from Marcus North. If she had intended to shoot him, she could have done it more easily at Pentstable.

When Lottie was summoned from Marcus' bedside,

she found her mother seated like royalty in one of the Gresham parlors, with a pretty parlormaid serving her tea and small cakes.

"Good morning, Mama," Lottie greeted her. "I expected you at Pomfret rather than here."

"They told me where you had gone. I wouldn't have known Evaline had I met her in London. She has changed much, but then, one does as one gets older. Good God!" she added as she took a full glance at her daughter. "What did you do to your hair?"

"A gentleman chopped it off with a razor," Lottie explained briefly.

Lady Forester closed her eyes. "I do not wish to hear any more about that. Also, I do not wish to know how Mr. North was shot, nor, in addition, do I wish to understand why that wild man drove out of this driveway—this very driveway, mind you!—when I was on my way to Pomfret, and nearly overturned my carriage."

The parlormaid had left the room. Lady Forester rose and placed her hands caressingly on her daughter's shoulders.

"I missed you, Lottie. Are you all right?"

"Yes, Mama." Lottie's smile was seraphic. "I should tell you that Marcus and I plan to marry. Soon." Noticing her mother's speculative expression, she laughed. "No, Mama. He did not even touch me."

Vastly relieved, Lady Forester let her hands drop. All seemed well with Lottie, and Lady Forester, who had realized almost too late how much affection she had for her daughter, saw to her great surprise that the girl no longer looked plain. Indeed, the thought came to the older woman that Lottie looked even beautiful!

But all she said, in a wry tone, was, "It would have been simpler, would it not, to have come downstairs to meet him at the start?"